Footprints in the Sand

ALSO BY MARY JANE CLARK

Footprints in the Sand

Mary Jane Clark

HARPER LUXE

An Imprint of HarperCollins*Publishers*

FOOTPRINTS IN THE SAND. Copyright © 2013 by Mary Jane Clark. All rights reserved. Printed in the United States of America. No part of this book may be used or reproduced in any manner whatsoever without written permission except in the case of brief quotations embodied in critical articles and reviews. For information address HarperCollins Publishers, 10 East 53rd Street, New York, NY 10022.

HarperCollins books may be purchased for educational, business, or sales promotional use. For information, please e-mail the Special Markets Department at SPsales@harpercollins.com.

FIRST HARPERLUXE EDITION

HarperLuxe™ is a trademark of HarperCollins Publishers

Library of Congress Cataloging-in-Publication Data is available upon request.

ISBN: 978-0-06-222282-4

13 14 ID/RRD 10 9 8 7 6 5 4 3 2 1

For Frances Mary Margaret McCormack Twomey,
with admiration, gratitude, and love.
Your friendship and loyalty have seen me through,
Francie. You are such a great gift.

And for all who struggle with Fragile X Syndrome,
as well as the researchers who are working on
treatments. We'll get there.

Prologue

She arrived twenty minutes early, parking in a spot where she could observe everyone entering and leaving the bar. Her hand shook as she twisted the key in the ignition to turn off the engine. Heart pounding, she settled back and began her vigil.

She wanted to meet him in a public place. That would be safer than going to his home or inviting him to hers. Having people around would ensure that he'd control himself. If he yelled or lashed out, there would be witnesses. He wouldn't want that.

Every muscle in her body tensed when she spotted him going into the bar. The door closed slowly behind him. She drew down the visor, flipped on the light, and checked her face in the mirror. She noted that she looked surprisingly calm.

She waited a few more minutes before getting out of the car. As she crossed the street, her long dark hair fanned over the shoulders of her yellow cotton sweater. She straightened her short skirt, took a deep breath, and pulled open the weathered door.

A group of guys were clustered in the entranceway. She felt their eyes sweeping over her but pretended not to notice. She was not going to let herself be distracted from her mission tonight.

Scanning the room, she saw the back of his head as he sat in a booth toward the rear of the bar, just where he'd said he'd be. She knew he wouldn't want people to recognize him talking to her. That was fine as far as she was concerned. She really didn't want to be seen with him either.

She made her way through the crowded space, ignoring the suggestive comments of some of the more loose-lipped customers. She was used to it. A few remarks she thought were flattering, but mostly she just found them irritating.

Sliding into the booth, she was grateful that it was a bit quieter in the rear of the room. What she had to say shouldn't be spoken loudly.

"What will it be?" he asked.

"One of those," she said, cocking her head in the direction of the mug on the table in front of him.

"Something to eat?"

"No," she said. "Not right now. I'm not really hungry."

He gestured for the waitress and ordered two more beers.

"So, Shelley," he said, leaning forward and looking into her eyes. "To what do I owe this honor?"

The smile disappeared from his face as she answered.

"I might as well get right to the point," she said. "People need to know what you've been up to."

Monday

You need not call the devil;
he'll come without calling.
AMISH PROVERB

Chapter 1

FEBRUARY 13 . . .
FIVE DAYS UNTIL THE WEDDING

Green-and-yellow birds chirped noisily in the palm trees outside the terminal at Sarasota Bradenton International Airport. The sky was clear and bright, but the breeze was cool as Piper Donovan and her parents pulled their luggage across the macadam.

"Not exactly beach weather," observed Piper, "but it's so much better than that frigid nightmare we left behind in New Jersey."

Terri smiled at her daughter. "Look at that sky," she said, gazing upward. "Did you ever see a more beautiful blue? And hardly a cloud in it."

"That's what you say every time we come down here, Terri," Vin remarked as his eyes scanned the parking lot, searching for the rental car.

"I know I do," said Terri. "That's because I can't ever get over how pretty it is. Heaven. Nora and Frank sure had the right idea when they moved down here."

"Too bad Uncle Frank didn't live long enough to really enjoy it," said Piper as she rested the small box she was carrying on top of the car. She reached for her parents' bags and hoisted them into the trunk. "I miss him."

"Me, too, sweetheart," said Terri as she thought of her older brother. "I wish he were still here, especially now. Frank should be walking his daughter down the aisle."

Vin reached out, put his arm around his wife's shoulder and drew her close. "Don't worry. I'm going to do the best I can to stand in for him," he said, kissing her on the forehead. "Even though there really isn't any aisle to walk down. Whatever happened to a church with a priest? Now, put on your sunglasses, Terri. You know the bright light bothers your eyes."

"This macular degeneration is such a drag," said Terri as she opened her purse.

While her mother searched for the glasses, Piper struggled to make the last bag fit. Vin scowled as he watched.

"Here, let me do it," he said, reaching into the trunk.

"I can do it, Dad."

"No, I'll do it."

Piper stood back, knowing that letting her father have his way was easier than resisting. After Vin had neatly rearranged the trunk's contents, Piper took the small box from the roof, holding it carefully as they all got into the sedan and buckled themselves into their seats.

"I'm glad Nora has finally met someone," said Terri as she settled back. "She's been by herself for too long."

"What's his name again?" asked Piper, pulling a clip from the pocket of her hoodie and sweeping her long blond hair up into a loose bun.

"Walter. Walter Engel."

"And what's his deal?"

"He's a businessman," answered Terri. "I gather he's into a lot of things. I know he owns the Whispering Sands Inn."

The car pulled out of the parking lot, exited the airport property, and turned left on the Tamiami Trail. All the passengers knew exactly where they were heading.

"My mouth is literally salivating for that pie already," said Piper, closing her eyes and resting her head on the rear seat.

The direct flight from New York to Sarasota left early in the morning, which meant rising well before dawn. The food on the plane had been next to nonexistent, leaving them famished. It was their custom on each yearly visit to their Florida relatives to stop first at Fisher's, an Amish restaurant, and get something to eat.

The gleaming office buildings and high-rise condominiums that overlooked the downtown marina gave way to a stretch of the Tamiami Trail dotted with chain stores and restaurants. At Bahia Vista Street, Vin steered left off the highway and toward the Amish section of town. Soon the houses became exceedingly modest, situated on tiny lots. Propane tanks outside signaled that the owners of the one-story cottages were determined to be "off the grid" and refused to use electricity.

The Pinecraft district of Sarasota was a winter vacation paradise for Plain People. The neighborhood had roughly two thousand year-round residents. The population more than doubled during the winter season, when Amish snowbirds descended from the North.

Piper stared intently out the car window, catching sight of a middle-aged woman wearing a starched white cap and a simple blue dress as she pedaled along the sidewalk on an adult-size tricycle. Her legs were covered in thick stockings, and she had on plain black shoes. The basket on the broad-seated trike was full of brown paper sacks.

"That's *so* not for me," said Piper, shaking her head in wonder as she watched the Amish woman pedal away.

Fisher's had three buildings. The largest, the restaurant, was flanked by a gift shop and a bakery-and-produce stand. The lunch crowd had already descended by the time the Donovans arrived and looked for a parking space. A line of waiting people snaked out the front door.

"Don't worry," said Vin. "It always moves pretty quickly."

"Can I check out the gift shop while you guys wait on line?" asked Piper as she placed the box she had held in her lap onto the rear seat next to her.

"Sure, go ahead," said Terri.

Inside the store Piper perused the merchandise. Amish cookbooks, handmade quilts and baskets, cloth dolls, and wooden toys were displayed alongside the traditional gift-shop fare of jewelry and T-shirts. At the left side of the room, Piper noticed a young man with a bowl-shaped haircut sitting at a long table. Large, gaily painted disks decorated the wall behind him. Each disk featured a different design and set of symbols. Birds, hearts, flowers, stars, trees, leaves, horses, cows, pine-apples, unicorns, and other symbols were arranged in all sorts of configurations.

Piper approached the table and watched as the young man painted a bright green shamrock in the middle of a blank disk. Feeling her eyes upon him, he looked up and smiled politely.

"Hi," said Piper, gesturing at the decorations on the wall. "Did you do all these?"

The young man nodded. "They're hex signs," he said. "Every symbol has a meaning."

"And each one conveys a kind of wish?" asked Piper as she began to recall the trip her family had taken to Hershey, Pennsylvania, one summer when she and her brother were little. She and Robert had been excited to go to the amusement park and walk the roads dotted with lampposts whose tops were shaped to look like silver-wrapped chocolate kisses. Her parents were more interested in the side trip to nearby Lancaster, where the Amish people drove their horse-drawn bug-gies. Piper vaguely remembered hearing about hex signs then.

The young man nodded again. "The one I'm paint-ing now portrays the good luck of the Irish."

"What about that one?" asked Piper, pointing to a sign featuring an American eagle.

"That one symbolizes strength and independence."

"And the one with the doves and the interlocking hearts?" asked Piper.

"That's a wedding hex sign. It proclaims a loving, happy marriage."

Piper studied the circle. A man's and a woman's names were printed in the center of the hearts. She hadn't gotten a gift for Kathy and Dan yet. Maybe this would be something special for them.

"Could you make another one of the marriage signs and put in the names of a different bride and groom?" she asked.

"Of course," said the young man. "I can have it ready in a few days."

When Piper gave the first names of the bride and groom, the young man looked up at her. "Kathy Leeds and Dan Clemens?" he asked.

"Yes. Do you know them?"

"Sure," he said in a soft voice that Piper had to strain to hear. "My sister works sometimes for Kathy's mother, and I know Dan from the Mote Marine Aquarium. I also know Kathy because I deliver pies and cakes to the hotel where she works."

"The Whispering Sands Inn?"

The young man nodded.

"My family and I are staying there while we're in town for the wedding," said Piper. "I hear it's beautiful. How could it not be when it's on that Siesta Key beach?"

At her remark, Piper could see the young man's facial expression change. His jaw clenched, and he turned his attention to writing down the order information. He didn't seem interested in any additional conversation.

As she left the gift shop, Piper felt satisfied yet slightly uneasy. Wasn't a hex a bad thing? Wasn't a hex a kind of curse?

Chapter 2

While he capped the tubes of paint and cleaned his brushes, Levi Fisher reflected on how different things were now. Just a few days ago, he would have been excited to have a commission to do a customized hex sign, especially one for a couple about to be married, a couple he knew to be such nice people. But since the awful thing had happened on the beach, he couldn't find enthusiasm for anything. He had been enveloped by a painful mental darkness.

As the child of Amish parents, Levi had been raised to live separate from the world and embrace instead his family and the Amish community. As an Amish adult, he would be expected to honor history and tradition, turn the other cheek, and lead a simple life through the practice of humility, modesty, thrift, and peacefulness.

It would always be his sacred duty to surrender to the will of God and submit to the authority of his Amish community and its rules. Setting rules and limits and respecting them were the keys to wisdom and fulfillment, and to becoming Christlike.

Living an Amish life required commitment. It wasn't something you were simply born into. It had to be something chosen. That's why, at the cusp of adulthood, Levi and others his age who'd been raised in Amish homes were given a choice: Were they going to accept the Amish faith as their own or turn their backs on it?

How could one be expected to make an informed, independent decision unless there were experiences of the outside world? *Rumspringa* was the Amish response to that question. From the Pennsylvania Dutch for "running around," *rumspringa* was a time when teenagers were allowed to relax the rules and know enough freedom to have their curiosity about the other world satisfied.

While Levi still lived at home and had all the same obligations and responsibilities as before, his parents and the church leaders had looked the other way as he'd been experimenting with his newfound freedom. He had tried smoking, which he hated. Alcohol tasted bad, but it left him feeling good at first until it left him feeling sick the next day. Still, it gave him courage to approach girls and work up the nerve to kiss them.

The private bedroom he'd been given allowed him to sneak out at night to meet up with friends or dates. He'd been taking full advantage of it. Until that night on the beach had gone so terribly wrong.

Levi looked up as the door to the gift shop opened. His sister entered, carrying a tray.

"I have brought your lunch," she said. "Your favorites. Chicken and dumplings and shoofly pie." She waited for Levi to clear a space on his worktable.

"Thank you, Miriam," said Levi, "but I am not hungry."

"What is the matter?" she asked. "Are you unwell?"

"I am fine. I am just not hungry."

Miriam stared at her younger brother. "Something is wrong, Levi. I know it is. You have not shown any appetite in the last few days, when you usually eat like a horse. And you have been walking around with the glummest expression on your face. What is wrong?"

"Nothing is wrong," said Levi.

"I do not believe you."

"Shh," said Levi, looking around the shop. "People can hear you."

"Come outside with me, then." Miriam put down the tray, turned, and walked out of the store. Levi reluctantly followed.

They found a secluded spot behind the shop. A stiff breeze whipped at the bottom of Miriam's blue cotton dress, and a wisp of brown hair blew free from beneath her cap. She wrapped her arms around herself, rubbing her hands up and down to keep warm. Her dark eyes stared directly into her brother's.

"I think I know what it is," she said. "I know why you are so preoccupied and worried."

Levi looked startled. "How could you possibly know?" he asked. "I have not told anybody."

"I know you so well, Levi. Go ahead, you can tell me. It will make it easier if you say it out loud."

She waited as her brother stood there, wringing his hands. She could tell he ached to unburden himself, yet he kept silent.

"All right," said Miriam. "I will say it for you."

"Do not say it," said Levi.

"Yes," she insisted. "It will not be the end of the world, Levi. I will always love you, no matter what."

Embarrassed and ashamed, Levi held his breath as he looked down at his shoes. Miriam reached out and took hold of her brother's arm.

"It is all right, Levi. It is all right if you have decided to make the break from us. It is all right if you do not feel you can make a lifelong commitment to our Amish ways. It is all right if you do not want to take the vows that will keep you forever separated from the world. You have to follow your heart, Levi. You have to do what *you* think is right. Uncle Isaac did it—you can, too. Even though I cannot see him anymore, it would not be the same with you. I would find a way."

Levi let out a deep sigh. "Is that what you thought?" he asked. "You could not be more wrong, Miriam. Never in my life have I been more certain that the Amish way is the life for me. I wish with all my heart that I had never, ever wandered."

Chapter 3

After consuming crab-cake sandwiches and sharing two huge pieces of Fisher's famous peanut-butter cream pie, Piper and her parents got back into the rental car and headed for Siesta Key, one of the barrier islands off the coast of Sarasota. Though they usually stayed with their relatives when they came down, Terri had insisted on checking into a hotel this time, knowing that there would be so much wedding-related activity going on. The last things either Nora or Kathy Leeds needed this week were houseguests. Kathy had booked them rooms at greatly reduced rates at the inn where she worked as an assistant manager.

"Welcome to Whispering Sands," said the attendant as he opened the car door. "I'll get your bags for you and have them sent to your rooms."

They entered through the double doorway to the Spanish-style villa and onto a spacious terra-cotta-tiled patio shaded by palm and papaya trees and edged with purple and pink bougainvillea. To the left of the patio was a large reception area furnished with rattan chairs and overstuffed sofas covered in lavender linen. Planters filled with purple dendrobium orchids were carefully placed around the room. Against the longest wall, there was a mosaic depicting a solitary white heron standing on one leg on the beach and serenely looking out at the blue-green water.

The mosaic had been inspired by the view at the far end of the patio. Acres of soft white sand led directly to the Gulf of Mexico and an open expanse of blue-green water. Big brown pelicans floated in the gently lapping surf. Sandpipers and plovers skittered across the sand.

"Look!" Piper pointed excitedly. "I saw a dolphin's fin bobbing out there."

"Are you sure it wasn't a shark?" asked Vin as he squinted to see.

"No, Dad," Piper said patiently. "It was a dolphin. Look! There it is again!"

All three of them stared transfixed as the creature emerged for air, then quickly dove beneath the surface again, its tail flapping in a salute before it disappeared.

"Isn't nature wonderful?" asked Terri.

"Amazing," said Piper.

A voice distracted them from the mesmerizing view. They turned to see a short blond woman with brilliant blue eyes walking toward them, her arms wide open and a bright smile on her face.

"You're here!" Kathy Leeds said, leaning forward to embrace her aunt. Piper noticed that her cousin looked thinner than the last time Piper had seen her, but she quickly wrote it off to typical bride shrinkage.

"How was your flight?" Kathy asked when the welcoming hugs and kisses were completed.

"It was fine," said Piper. "But getting up at five A.M. is brutal."

Vin nodded. "Especially when you leave things to the last minute and stay up until one in the morning packing."

"I know," said Piper. "I'm going to get around to being more organized." She grinned, knowing she'd made that promise before.

Terri reached out to take her niece's hand. "Robert and Zara wanted me to tell you again how sorry they are to miss the wedding, Kathy. Zara is having such miserable morning sickness."

Piper spoke up. "It's not just morning. It's all day long. Some days she barely gets out of bed." Her tone betrayed some skepticism at her sister-in-law's behavior. Zara could be so dramatic, thought Piper. And not in a good way.

"Well, we'll miss them both," said Kathy, "but we understand. You must be so excited about a new baby in the family."

"Oh, we are," said Terri, smiling so broadly that her eyes squinted almost shut. "I can't wait to be a grandmother."

"Now, your rooms are all ready for you if you want to get settled in and take a nap," said Kathy. "Mom is having dinner for us at her place tonight. We're just so glad you're here."

As they walked back through the reception area, Piper pointed to the mosaic. "That is so beautiful," she said. "Look at the intricate workmanship."

"It is, isn't it? We used to have another one, a companion piece with sea turtles, but it was stolen," said Kathy. "Actually, we've had a number of thefts in the last few months."

Chapter 4

Cryder Robbins, M.D., smiled with satisfaction as he straightened the row of small ivory figurines on his desk. He had quite a collection of netsuke now, begun when he'd first traveled to Japan some years ago and continued ever since. He was interested only in the ones made before ivory from elephants became illegal. Netsuke cut from woven cane, lacquered wood, clay, or nutshells held no excitement for him.

Cryder picked up the carved figure of Hotei, the legendary god of happiness and abundance, and rubbed its fat, round belly. It was the first netsuke he'd bought, paying just a few hundred dollars for it. And it certainly had brought him good luck. His medical practice was thriving, so much so that he could well afford to pay for more valuable figurines now. Depending on rarity, artistry, and age, there were netsuke for which Cryder was willing to pay thousands.

Turning to his computer, he entered the Internet address for the Web site of his favorite netsuke gallery. He had his eye on a full-moon rabbit, carved in a perfect sphere and signed by the artist over three hundred years ago. In Asian folklore, female rabbits conceive through the touch of the full moon's light, or by crossing water by moonlight, or by licking moonlight from a male rabbit's fur. Often weary of the scientific nature of his profession, Cryder was drawn to the whimsy captured in these prized figurines.

The dealer wanted sixteen thousand dollars for the full-moon rabbit. Cryder was admiring the image and considering whether he should go for it when there was a knock on the office door.

"Come in," he called, clicking to make the computer screen go blank.

His wife poked her head into the office. "Busy morning," she said, smiling brightly as she walked in and took a seat in the chair across the desk. Small and trim from her careful diet and morning walks on the beach, she sat up straight.

"Yes, Umiko," he said. "Very productive." He scratched the deep cleft in his chin, the one Umiko said made him look like Michael Douglas.

"Your next appointment isn't until two o'clock. Want to go out and have lunch?" she asked.

He loved Umiko, and even though it had been his idea, having her work as his receptionist could get to be too much. Sometimes he felt stifled by the excessive togetherness. But Umiko had been loyal to him all these years, and he trusted her implicitly.

"Sure," he said, standing up and shedding his lab coat. "Where do you want to go?"

"Someplace where we can get something light," said Umiko as she pushed a strand of jet-black hair behind her ear. "We have dinner at Nora Leeds's tonight, and I know she'll go all out."

Cryder's tanned brow furrowed as he let out a deep sigh. "The dinner and that cruise and the Jungle Gardens trip—we're expected to do all that and then go to the wedding and reception, too? It's a bit much, Umiko, isn't it?"

"It is an honor to be invited, Cryder," Umiko said softly. "It would be disrespectful not to attend."

Chapter 5

Once Terri and Vin were settled in their sooth-ing, aquatic-themed room, Kathy escorted Piper to hers. Piper towered over her cousin as they walked down the long corridor to the very end of the building.

"The room is smaller than your parents', but it's my favorite," said Kathy as she opened the door.

"This is great," Piper said enthusiastically, look-ing inside. A queen-size bed covered with fluffy white pillows and a down comforter dominated the space. A large flat-screen TV hung on the opposite wall. An upholstered chair and a small desk sat at the side. Tucked into an alcove at the rear of the room were a closet and a chest of drawers.

Piper walked across the room to inspect the bath-room. A large soaking tub sat beneath a picture window. She peered out and squealed with delight.

"Are you kidding? My own private pool?" she asked.

Kathy nodded, smiling. "Come on. Let's go out there."

At the rear of the suite, a door led out to a small, secluded garden. The wooden walls were tall enough that no one without a ladder could possibly see over them. In the corner a small fountain surrounded by orange hibiscus sprayed water into the air. Two padded lounge chairs sat on soft white sand adjacent to the compact lap pool.

"There's a retractable awning," said Kathy, pointing to a switch by the door. "I know how you hate the sun."

"Uh, this is everything," said Piper as she plopped down on a lounge chair. "I'm never leaving."

"I thought you'd like it," said Kathy with satisfaction. She lowered herself into the other chair and put up her feet. "Nothing but the best for my maid of honor."

"Wait a minute," said Piper as she got up and headed inside again. "I have something I want to show you."

When she returned, Piper held the little box she'd carried on her lap during the plane ride. Now she opened the lid.

"Look at this," she said as she pulled out a delicate white circle and held it up with her long, slender fingers.

"A sand dollar?" asked Kathy.

"Yes, but I didn't find it on the beach. I made it and the other ones in here from sugar. They're going to decorate your wedding cake."

"Oh, Piper!" Kathy exclaimed, her eyes glistening. "How beautiful!"

Piper studied her cousin's face. The two of them had known each other all their lives, having been born only three months apart, and while Kathy was smiling now, Piper sensed something else. Was it tension? Worry? Fear?

"So how's it going?" she asked. "Are you flipping out yet? I remember when I was planning *my* wedding. I thought I'd go out of my mind. And I didn't even get anywhere near the final days."

Kathy looked with sympathy at Piper. "How are *you*?" she asked. "I can't tell you how much I admire the way you handled everything, Piper. That had to be so rough."

"Yeah, it was pretty devastating at first," said Piper as she reached over and ran her fingers through the sand. "But I realized I was more embarrassed by the cancellation than sad about the fact that Gordon and I weren't going to be married. Now I know it was for the best. By breaking off the engagement, he really ended up doing me a huge favor."

"How so?" asked Kathy. "You loved him, didn't you?"

Piper considered the question. "I did, or at least I thought I did. But whenever I think about him now, I have this feeling of relief. We really didn't have what it takes to go the distance. Not like you and Dan."

Kathy laid her head against the lounge chair's pillow and looked up at the sky. "I'm lucky, Piper, and I know it. Lucky to be totally sure that Dan is the one for me. I want to spend the rest of my life with him. Now, if we can just get through the wedding."

"So many details and decisions, right?"

"Most of those have been taken care of by now," said Kathy. "You know how organized my mother is. She's been great."

"Then what's the problem?" asked Piper.

Kathy looked at Piper with distress. "Shelley Hart, a girl who works with me here at the inn, has become one of my best friends, and I asked her to my brides-maid. No one has seen or heard from her for the last three days."

Chapter 6

Whenever he had something weighing on his mind, Dan Clemens stole away from his office and went to the turtle tank to spend some time with Hang Tough. The green sea turtle had come to the Mote Marine Lab with a serious head wound and a fishing hook in one eye. Though blinded, the giant turtle thrived now in a floor-to-ceiling viewing tank, fed daily with squid, lettuce, and other vegetables. Officials determined that Hang Tough would be better off living at Mote than being returned to the wild. Meanwhile visitors were given the opportunity to learn about the issues that sea turtles faced.

As Dan watched the turtle glide though the water, he marveled, as he always did. Hang Tough had been in the tank for two decades. For years and years, he floated and dove and climbed and swam, seemingly at peace. He didn't have to search for food or worry about predators, animal or human. He appeared to be utterly content. But who could really know what went on in Hang Tough's mind?

"Ouch!" Dan winced as the turtle bumped into the hard wall, his nose bouncing against the side of the tank. "Careful there, big fella."

Hang Tough turned and swam on, apparently undisturbed. Dan ran his hand through his sun-streaked hair and wished he could take setbacks and bumps in the road of life the way that turtle could.

Dan already had the world's best job. Working as a marine biologist at Mote was something he'd always dreamed of doing. Growing up in Sarasota, Dan had a permanent tan, and his ash-blond hair was brightened by the sun. He'd been passionate about the Gulf of Mexico and its wildlife and ecosystems since he was a young boy. He had completed the necessary courses in chemistry, zoology, biology, physics, and mathematics and had interned at Mote when he was in college. After graduate school he'd obtained the position he now held.

Mote had also led him to the woman he loved. He met Kathy when she signed up as one of the hundreds of volunteers who patrolled Sarasota's thirty-five miles of beaches during the sea turtles' nesting season in May through October. Soon he would marry her.

Dan didn't want anything to mar the happiness of his wedding day, especially not Shelley Hart's disappearance. Kathy had been nonchalant at first. Shelley could be a little forgetful about a lunch or dinner date, and she might neglect to call if she was going to be late for work. But by the second day, Kathy had become concerned when repeated phone calls went unanswered. After driving over to Shelley's condo several times and finding no one there, Kathy was now downright afraid.

Dan didn't want her to worry about anything this close to the big day. At the same time, if Shelley wasn't able to be in the wedding party, that was all right with him. He'd always felt funny about the prospect anyway. There was something uncomfortable about having a former girlfriend stand at the altar as you promised to love, honor, and cherish someone else.

Chapter 7

The sound of her cell phone woke Piper from her nap. She glanced at the screen. It was her mother.

"Aunt Nora wants us at her place at six," said Terri. "We'll meet you in the parking lot a few minutes before that."

"Why are we driving? It's close enough to just walk up the beach," said Piper as she stretched out on the soft sheets.

"I know," said Terri. "But I have some things I want to take over, and I'm not trudging through the sand like a bedouin."

Piper glanced at the clock and calculated how long she needed to take a shower, wash her hair, and get ready.

"You guys go ahead," she said. "I'll be right behind you."

"All right," said Terri. "But please, Piper, don't start the trip by being late for dinner. It's disrespectful."

"Mom. I'm twenty-seven years old."

Willing herself to get out of bed, Piper was glad to be going to the dinner party. She just wished it were going to be later. She would have loved to grab some more sleep. Feeling tired and not particularly perky, she was determined to rally. This was Kathy's time, and the last thing Piper wanted to be was a drag.

After a shower and shampoo, she rummaged through her duffel bag and selected a short black skirt and a silk scoop-necked blouse in a blue-and-black paisley print. She pulled her wet hair into a ponytail and put on a pair of dangling silver earrings. After applying a little lip gloss and some mascara, she slipped on a pair of ballet flats. Piper went out the door and down the hall, sliding her cell phone into her pocket.

After she walked through the reception area and out to the patio, she had a decision to make. Turn one way to the sidewalk that would lead down the road to Aunt Nora's town house or turn the other way and stroll up the beach. Practicality versus beauty. Beauty won. The ballet flats came off.

The sand was powdery and cool beneath her bare feet, and she remembered that Sarasota's white sands were quartz-based. Even on a blistering day, the sand didn't get too hot. When Piper reached the water's edge, she stuck her toes in, then quickly pulled them out again.

"Cold, isn't it?"

Startled, she spun in the direction of the voice. A tall, athletic-looking guy with dark curly hair was standing behind her. He was wearing a black wet suit and balancing a red kayak on his shoulder. She noticed part of a tattoo peeking out from the cuff of the wet suit. Piper saw his eyes sweep over her body.

"Are you actually going in?" she asked.

"Yeah, I want to squeeze in some exercise before it gets dark."

Piper watched as the man lowered the kayak onto the sand, his leg and arm muscles rippling beneath the tight-fitting rubber. "I've never ridden in a kayak," she said. "It looks like fun."

"You should try it sometime," said the man. "It's easier and safer than a canoe. And it's a great way to tour the area. There's some pretty spectacular scenery and wildlife around here, free for everybody. You'd like it."

"Maybe I will while I'm here," said Piper.

"I run the kayak and paddleboard rental place over there," he said, nodding in the direction of a wooden pavilion farther up the beach. "Stop by and I'll give you a lesson. You're vacationing, right?"

"Actually, I'm here for a wedding. I've been coming down here for years, though. My aunt lives in one of those condos." She pointed.

"Oh, yeah? Who's your aunt?"

"Nora Leeds," said Piper.

"You're kidding me."

Piper smiled. "So that would mean you know her, right?"

"Actually, I know her daughter, Kathy. She's marrying a good friend of mine, Dan Clemens. In fact, I'm his best man."

Piper's eyes widened. "And I'm Kathy's maid of honor!"

"Whoa! That's amazing." The man offered his hand. "I'm Brad. Brad O'Hara."

"Piper Donovan," she said. "I guess we'll be spending some time together this week."

"All of a sudden, this wedding looks like it's going to be a lot more fun." Brad grinned.

Or was it a leer? Though her first inclination was to like a friend of Kathy's fiancé, Piper felt vaguely uncomfortable as this guy looked at her.

"I suppose you're on your way to the dinner party," Brad continued. "I was going to blow it off, but maybe I'll be able to stop by after all."

As she drew close to the waterfront town house, Piper could see that a crowd was already gathered on the lanai. Cocktails in hand, they were enjoying a breathtaking bright orange sun as it lowered over the horizon. Piper snapped a picture of it with her iPhone.

"There she is," called Vin. "And not that late after all."

Piper smiled and kissed everyone she knew on the cheek. She stopped at the florid-faced, middle-aged man standing near the sliding glass door. His hair was cut close to his head, in an effort, Piper suspected, to make him appear more youthful and camouflage the fact that his hairline had receded. He wore obviously expensive clothes, and Piper caught the scent of what she recognized as Obsession as she shook his hand.

"Piper, I want you to meet Walter, my friend," said Nora. Piper's aunt wore a brightly flowered caftan and bejeweled high-heeled sandals, and as she said this, she moved closer to the man at her right. She was beaming as she spoke. "Walter recently bought the inn where you and your parents are staying."

"Nora tells me you're an actress, Piper. What would I have seen you in?" asked Walter as he held the handshake a little too long.

"I don't know if you watch soap operas, but I had a recurring role in *A Little Rain Must Fall*."

"I'm afraid I didn't catch that."

Piper thought she heard some condescension in the man's tone. Or maybe she was just looking for it. It had become a natural reflex to brace herself when she talked about her acting career. Most people were eager to inquire about it, but very few understood what the industry was really like. Even after five years of actively pursuing her career, Piper constantly found herself confronted by the realities of a life in show business. She had decided that most people fell into one of two categories: those who thought acting was wonderful and applauded her for her efforts and those who thought she should get a real job. To the latter group, acting, unless at the highest-paying, household-name levels, wasn't a legitimate way to make a living.

She was hoping that Walter Engel wasn't going to be a member of the second group. Piper wanted to like the man her aunt seemed so happy about. Nora *had* been alone for a long time, and Piper thought it would be great for her to have somebody to love.

She tried again. "Actually, I just shot a dog-food commercial that will start airing next month."

"Great," said Walter. "I'm going to watch for that."

He seemed genuine enough this time, but Piper desperately wanted to change the subject to something other than herself.

"Anyway, I love my room at your inn," she said. "That little private garden with the pool is awesome."

"You like that, do you?" asked Walter. "I hope we can keep it."

"What do you mean?"

"We're going to be expanding, and since that room and garden is at the very end of the building, it might have to be knocked out so we can build on from there. Right now I'm waiting to see the architect's plans."

"Oh, no, you can't do that!" Piper protested. "It's so great the way it is."

She felt an arm wrap around her shoulder. It was her cousin.

"Hey, Pipe, you aren't telling my boss what to do, are you? Enough, now," said Kathy, smiling. "I want you to meet Dr. Robbins and his wife, Umiko. Dr. Robbins took good care of Daddy before he died. They have become such good friends of our family. And I want to introduce you to Isaac Goode, our wedding planner."

As Piper let her cousin steal her away, she heard the doorbell ring. She looked up to see Brad O'Hara standing at the door. He had obviously decided to skip his kayak ride.

Chapter 8

Miriam took the tray of cheese puffs out of the oven and slid a glass casserole dish into its place. With a spatula she transferred the canapés to the silver serving piece she had polished for Mrs. Leeds the day before. With the wedding fast approaching, Mrs. Leeds had several hours of work for her to do every day. Miriam was glad to juggle her schedule to accommodate her favorite employer.

Before going out to the living room to pass the hors d'oeuvres, Miriam measured out the appropriate amount of water to cook the rice and set it to boil. As she put the lid on the pot, she sensed somebody else in the kitchen.

"Hello, Miriam."

Immediately recognizing the voice, she didn't turn around.

"You're looking well," he said. "I was watching inside as you served everyone. You do a very nice job. If you ever need work, just give me a call. I can always use somebody like you."

Miriam adjusted her apron as she tried to ignore Isaac.

He reached out and gently took hold of her forearm. "Come on, Miriam," he pleaded. "This is ridiculous. Your brother understands. Why can't you?"

She pulled her arm away and twisted around to face him. "I know that Levi sees you, Isaac, even though he should not. I do not say a word, but I cannot have anything to do with you, and you know it. You made your decision, and now you have to live with the consequences."

Isaac took a step back, stung by the vehemence in her voice. He let out a long, deep sigh as his facial expression grew dark. Then, as he stood there, he felt a sense of growing rage.

"That's just crazy, Miriam," he whispered angrily, his clenched fist coming down firmly on the counter. "I'm your uncle, your flesh and blood. We have the same color hair, the same dark eyes, the same dimples, and the same crooked bottom teeth. We were raised with the same Amish values. The only thing I did was follow my own conscience. For that I have to be punished for the rest of my life?"

"You know the rules, Uncle Isaac."

"The rules are antiquated and inhumane."

"You see it as you will. But just because Levi has taken pity on you, do not look for that from me. Levi is too soft for his own good." She picked up the serving platter and walked right past him and out of the kitchen.

Isaac stood there, staring after her. "I know he is," he said quietly. "I know he is."

Chapter 9

During the buffet dinner of sweet-and-sour chicken, saffron rice, and asparagus, the conversation was upbeat. Talk centered on wedding plans and festivities. Tomorrow Kathy and Piper were going downtown for dress fittings, and Nora had theater tickets. Wednesday there would be a cruise and a picnic on Sarasota Bay. Thursday a trip to Jungle Gardens was scheduled, and Terri and Piper would bake the wedding cake. The decorating would be done on Friday. Dan's parents were hosting a rehearsal dinner that evening, the night before the wedding.

"Although Isaac would have you think otherwise, there isn't much to rehearse," said Dan. "We simply want to stand on the beach Saturday morning near the turtle nests at the hour we first met and say our vows to each other." He took his fiancée's hand and brought it to his lips.

"I think that's so romantic, isn't it? If it weren't for those sea turtles coming up and laying their eggs in the sand, you two might never have connected," said Piper. "Destiny."

Her father frowned and shook his head. "I'd call it a coincidence. Totally random."

"I don't know about that, Uncle Vin," said Kathy. "When you think about the fact that the mother sea turtles, after traveling the oceans of the world for twenty or thirty years, return in the middle of the night to lay their eggs on the very beach where they themselves were hatched, you've got to believe in some sort of cosmic plan. It's a miracle that all those years later, the turtles can remember and find those beaches. That's no coincidence. I like to think that Dan and I were destined to meet, that the turtles were the instruments that brought us together."

"Exactly." Piper sighed. "It's so romantic."

Vin shrugged, his attention diverted by the pies that the young Amish woman placed on the buffet table.

"Thank you, Miriam," said Nora. "Come have some pie from Fisher's, everyone. Except for the key lime pie, Vin. *I* made that one especially for you. I know how much you love it."

"Yours is the best I've ever had, Nora."

"And it's the easiest thing to make, too," said Nora as she sliced into the pie. "I got the recipe years ago from a magazine. I can't even count the number of times I've made it. Walter loves it, too."

Kathy put her hand up. "None for me."

Piper had noticed that her cousin hadn't eaten much of her dinner either. "Do you feel okay, Kath?" she asked.

"I'm fine," said Kathy softly. "I just wish I knew where Shelley was. I'm so worried about her."

"I checked with the sheriff's department again before I came over here," said Walter. "They said they've issued a missing-persons alert for her, but nothing so far. They said that odds are she'll turn up."

Vin sat up straighter. "What's all this about?" he asked, his years as a New York cop kicking into gear.

"Shelley is a friend of Kathy's," Piper explained. "Kathy hasn't been able to reach her for the last few days."

"And she hasn't come in to work either," Walter added. "I'm really feeling it. I depend on her for so much."

Tears of frustration welled in Kathy's eyes. "I just don't think the police are paying enough attention. They don't seem to take this seriously. I'm really worried about what's happened to her. Not to mention she's supposed to be in our wedding in a few days."

"Was her car gone?" asked Vin. "Were her purse and keys left in her house?"

"Her car, purse, and keys weren't there," said Kathy.

"Well," said Vin, "that could indicate she left of her own volition. Unless there's evidence of foul play, the cops aren't going to get too excited. They'll take the report and maybe put a description of the car in the National Crime Information Center database, but it doesn't mean they're going to roll out a team and start interviewing all the neighbors and acquaintances. The report will sit in a file, and you might get a couple of calls asking if she's come home yet, but that's about it. They figure an adult is allowed to come and go as she pleases."

"I don't care," said Kathy, pushing back her chair. "I'm calling the sheriff again."

When her daughter had left the room, Nora spoke in a low voice. "Roz Golubock told me something this afternoon," she said. "Something I haven't shared with Kathy, because she's already so upset."

The other guests leaned forward.

"What? What did she say?" asked Dan. "Kathy doesn't need one more thing right now."

"I know," said Nora. "But Roz told me she saw a man carrying something into the vegetation at the end of the property a few nights ago."

"Carrying what?" asked Vin sharply.

"Roz wasn't absolutely sure, but she thought it could have been a woman's body."

No one spoke as the group digested the information.

Finally Dr. Robbins broke the silence. "Forgive me, Nora, but Roz is eighty-seven years old and her eyesight isn't always the best," he said. "I'm not saying she didn't see something. I'm just inclined to take her report with a grain of salt."

"All the same," said Vin, "the police should be informed."

When she returned, Kathy's face was pale, and she was trembling as she sat down at the table.

"What?" asked Dan, taking hold of her arm. "What did they say?"

"Shelley's car." Kathy's voice cracked. "The police found her car at the Sarasota Square Mall. There was blood on the seat. And they asked about Shelley's next of kin. All of a sudden, they're paying attention."

Chapter 10

Levi waited until it was dark before he snuck out. Though *rumspringa* allowed him to come and go at will, he didn't want to answer any questions tonight. He couldn't possibly respond truthfully. There was no way he could tell his parents that he was going to Siesta Beach to the spot where Shelley was buried.

He took his bicycle from the shed and quietly rolled it down the short driveway. He hopped on and began to pedal out to Bahia Vista Street.

As he turned west, cars sped by him on the heavily trafficked road. The thought crossed his mind that one might strike him and put him out of his misery. It would be a relief. Then there would be no question about what to do. The secret would die with him.

When he reached the Tamiami Trail, he stopped to wait for the light to change. A black pickup truck careened around the corner, its muffler firing noisily. The driver stuck his head through the open window.

"Watch out, you Ah-mo!" he yelled at Levi.

Levi felt his face grow hot. It wasn't that he hadn't heard the slur before. His dress, his hair, his differentness—they all caused some people to react in less than kind ways. But tonight he just couldn't deal with what three days ago he would have taken in stride. He felt a tear roll down his cheek.

He pedaled onward. When he got to the North Bridge, he stopped to watch the fishermen cast their lines over the side. He inspected their big plastic buckets, piled high with redfish and sheepshead.

Finally he got to Ocean Boulevard. There were no streetlights, and the only illumination came from the headlights of passing cars and the lamps inside the houses and condominium complexes set back from the road. Levi came to a stop, got off the bike, and hid it in a hedge of sea grapes. He took the flashlight from his rear pocket and walked the rest of the way to the beach.

As he listened to the rhythmic sound of the crashing waves hitting the shore again and again, he recalled all the times he had walked this beach. The happiness and excitement he'd found here. The summers spent keeping track of the turtle nests, watching in May,

June, and July as the number of nests grew week by week. Waiting for them to hatch in August, September, and October. The year-round fun he had fishing with Uncle Isaac. The shells and sand dollars he'd collected with his sister.

Miriam.

If you tell anyone what you saw, I'll kill your sister.

The words reverberated in Levi's head. He felt his throat tighten.

He wanted to tell the police. Levi knew that was the right thing to do. But he couldn't take the chance of putting Miriam in mortal danger.

Levi reached the spot. His heart beat faster as he trained his flashlight on the sand. Three days of breezes and sea spray had erased all signs that a deep hole had been dug there.

The last burial he'd been to had taken place three days after his aunt Rachel's death. So many members of their Amish community had been involved. Some helped with preparing the body. Others built the plain wooden coffin. Some sat with the body while the grave was hand-dug as a sign of love and respect. Several hundred people had attended Aunt Rachel's funeral.

Shelley had missed that care and attention. Levi tried desperately to rationalize that at least Shelley's grave had been hand-dug. Had that given her some small amount of dignity?

He wished he could turn back the clock. He wished he had never gone out that night, that he hadn't had those beers at the bar in Siesta Village, that he hadn't gone for that walk on the beach to sober himself up. But the beach had always been his friend, the place he came to think things through and marvel at the wonder of nature.

That night he'd been struggling with his decision about his future in the Amish world. Tonight Levi was struggling with something far more dangerous, far more sinister. He hoped that coming to the place where it had happened would help him decide what to do.

Levi knelt beside the grave. As he prayed, his tears began to flow, building into racking sobs.

Slowly he got to his feet. As he walked away, Levi reached into his pocket, pulled out his handkerchief, and mopped his face. He didn't realize that his cell phone had slipped out as well and had fallen into the sand.

If you tell anyone what you saw, I'll kill your sister.

The man who had killed Shelley Hart and stuffed her body into a sandy hole was clearly capable of carrying through on that threat.

Chapter 11

The evening's festive atmosphere dissolved as the diners talked about the discovery of Shelley's bloodstained car.

"Shelley was sweet and generous and would do anything for you," said Kathy, her voice trembling. "She was such a good friend to me."

"Honey, don't talk in the past tense yet," said Dan. "We don't know what's really happened."

"That's right," said Brad as he sat back in his chair and cracked his knuckles. "Under Shelley's sweet exterior is a will of iron. Take it from somebody who knows—she's a force to be reckoned with, and I'd never bet against her."

"I feel like we should be doing something," said Piper as she and her parents got into the car to return to the inn. "Maybe we should go down to the sheriff's office."

Her father shook his head as he glanced in the rearview mirror. "Do you have anything to help the investigation?" he asked.

"Not really," answered Piper quietly.

"Well, then you have to let them do their jobs," said Vin.

A few moments passed in an uncomfortable silence. Piper stared at the back of her father's head, noting how white his hair had gotten. She wondered if it was genetic or due to all the worrying he did anticipating every possible disaster—and if she, too, was destined to go gray early.

"I thought Walter seemed very nice, didn't you?" asked Terri, changing the subject.

"He was all right," said Vin. "His handshake wasn't the firmest—and neither was that wedding planner's."

"Stop it, Vin. Don't tell me that you're going to judge Walter by his handshake," said Terri. "Nora thinks he's wonderful, and she's always been a good judge of character. She told me that he's so generous with local charities, always donating money or purchasing tables at fund-raisers. Nora is buying cocktail dresses for the first time since Frank died. If he makes her happy, I don't care how weak his handshake is."

"Being generous to local charities is good business," said Vin as they pulled out of the gravel driveway.

"You are *so* cynical, Vin. Give the guy a break, will you?"

"I'm not cynical," protested Vin. "I'm just realistic. Some of these guys don't give a rat's ass about doing good. They only want the publicity and a chance to hobnob with others just like themselves."

"How did she meet Walter anyway?" asked Piper absentmindedly from the backseat. She was still thinking about Kathy's missing friend. *What if that old lady really saw what she claimed? Can there be some sort of connection?*

"Actually, she met him through Shelley," said Terri. "Shelley knocked on her door one day, introduced herself as Walter's representative, and asked if Nora would consider selling her town house," said Terri. "Apparently Walter's interested in buying all ten of the condos in the development, since the property adjoins his. He has big plans for the inn. Shelley would make the initial contact, and then Walter was the closer."

"So Nora's going to sell to him?" asked Vin.

"At first she thought absolutely not," answered Terri. "But now I think she's seriously considering it. Between the three of us, I think Nora is hoping that she and Walter will get married."

"And then she'd live with him somewhere else?" asked Piper.

"Mm-hmm. Apparently he's building a house for himself at the other end of the Whispering Sands property."

Vin steered the rental car into the inn's parking lot. As they got out of the sedan, a clap of thunder resounded through the night air.

Piper shivered involuntarily as she looked toward the dark vegetation that separated the inn from the condominiums.

Did somebody really carry a woman's body in there?

Chapter 12

After the dinner party, Isaac Goode drove off Siesta Key and headed toward downtown Sarasota. A few raindrops hit the windshield as he parked his car in the condominium's parking lot.

When Isaac entered his apartment, he carefully placed his keys on the small table just inside the front door, trying to make as little noise as possible. He didn't want to wake up Elliott.

Without turning on the lights, Isaac tiptoed across the living room, slid open the glass door, and stepped onto the balcony. He stared up into the dark sky, waiting to see the flickering of lightning bolts. So far there were none. Just the sound of rumbling in the distance. But weather systems moved fast in Florida. The forecaster on the radio had said that the storm would be traveling west, out into the Gulf. That meant it was coming their way.

There was nothing Isaac liked more than a good storm. The demonstration of nature's power excited him. It was the ultimate show, too vast for any human being to orchestrate. Isaac appreciated all the elements that had come together: hot air drawn into the atmosphere; fierce, gusting winds; storm clouds rolling and tumbling high above the earth; jagged lightning cutting through the sky; and the booming thunder that punctuated the display. Isaac was in awe of the Supreme Being who'd designed all that.

The lights flipped on behind him, and he spun around.

"Elliott! You scared me to death!" he exclaimed when he saw who it was.

"I could say the same thing, Isaac. I heard the sliding door and thought we were being robbed."

"I'm sorry. I was trying to be quiet."

"That's okay. I really couldn't sleep with all this thunder."

Where Isaac was dark and of average height, Elliott was fair and tall. They were both in their late thirties and had been together for almost five years. From the moment they'd met, they'd found it easy to talk to each other.

"How was dinner, by the way?" Elliott asked.

"Oh, it was fine, I guess. My niece was there," Isaac said as he turned and took a few steps toward the railing. With his back to Elliott, he spoke into the darkness. "She's still shunning me."

Wrapping his bathrobe closer to his chest, Elliott stepped up behind his partner. "I'm so sorry, Isaac. I know how hurtful that all is."

In spite of everything that had happened—or maybe because of it—Isaac still believed in God. Rejecting an Amish life and failing to be a walking billboard for religion didn't mean he loved God any less. It was God who had seen him through. Until he'd met Elliott, there was nothing to rely on, no family to assist when times were hard and jobs got scarce. Isaac had known he would be shunned; he just didn't realize how cruel and painful it would actually be. Tonight's conversation with Miriam had been a prime example of that.

"It would have been better if I'd just walked away after my *rumspringa*. But I didn't have the courage."

"Isaac, it was way more complicated than you let on. You didn't want to leave your family and friends. It was natural for you to fear leaving behind the only world you knew. And you had your parents to think of."

"Yeah, I know," Isaac said.

Twenty years ago, when he was Levi's age, Isaac had gone ahead with the formal religious-instruction classes and eliminated all the trappings of *rumspringa* from his life. He'd stopped going to parties. He'd sold the used car, donated his video games to Goodwill, and gotten rid of the T-shirts he'd collected while he navigated and enjoyed the outside world. Despite his misgivings, he'd prepared to be baptized into the Amish faith.

"Even as the bishop was placing his hands on my head, I knew I was making a mistake. I wanted to yell and run away. But what did I do? I kept silent."

"And you tried to make the best of it, Isaac." Elliott hugged his partner. "You tried as hard as anyone could, but you had to leave in order to be yourself."

If Isaac had just rejected baptism, it would have been much better. Those who refused to become part of the church were allowed to go and create a new life of their own. But, once baptized, members were bound to the Amish faith for the rest of their lives. Breaking the vow he'd made meant that Isaac had to be shunned by the entire community.

No one could eat with him. No one could accept gifts from him. No one could do business with him. His parents, sister, and four brothers hadn't spoken to him since he'd left, nor had any of his old friends. They didn't want to associate with someone who hadn't followed the rules.

"After all these years, the only one who's dared to have a relationship with me is Levi. And he's had to sneak around, meeting me on the beach to go fishing. It was so awful hearing his sister, Miriam, tell me that she plans on shunning me forever."

Staring down at the silhouettes of pleasure boats bobbing in the marina, Isaac said a silent prayer of thanks. He'd built a successful career through creativity and hard work. He had Elliott and friends, a nice place to live, and some money in the bank.

"Let's turn in," Elliott coaxed.

As they walked through the living room, Elliott looked over at the long expanse above the sofa. Sea turtles made up of tiny pieces of polished stone shimmered in the lamplight.

"God, I love that mosaic."

Chapter 13

Piper let herself into the room and immediately went to the window and opened it. She loved hearing the waves of the Gulf of Mexico relentlessly rushing in and out. Though the occasional pounding thunder interrupted, the steady roar of the surf was soothing.

She unpacked the contents of her rolling duffel bag and hung her clothes in the closet. Then she undressed, washed her face, and brushed her teeth. Climbing into bed, she took out her iPhone and listened to her messages. There was only one she wanted to return right away. It was Jack Lombardi's.

"Hey, Pipe. It's me. Just thinking of you and wondering if you got down there all right. Give me a call when you can. Miss you already."

As she called the New York number, Piper realized she was smiling. Jack answered after the second ring. She could hear the enthusiasm and pleasure in his voice.

"Hi, you! How's it going down there?"

"So far, so good," said Piper. "We got here in one piece. The weather was beautiful today—sunny, although a little too cool for the beach. But a storm is starting now."

"And your parents?"

"They're my parents, Jack. You know how they are."

"Not really, Pipe. I only know what you've told me about them."

"Well, lucky you. That's about to change, isn't it?"

"Can't wait," said Jack. "I'm gonna catch that flight on Friday."

"I'll be at the airport to pick you up. I think you're going to love it here, Jack. The hotel is beautiful. Kathy has booked you a room."

"Next to yours, I hope."

She smiled. "Having my parents right down the hall complicates things."

"I love a challenge," answered Jack. "Remember, I'm professionally trained in undercover operations."

They chatted for few more minutes. Jack told her what he could about a case he was working on. It wasn't much. He was careful not to reveal anything sensitive or confidential about his counterterrorism work at the FBI. Finally Piper told him about the dinner at her aunt's place and her cousin's missing friend.

"Why are you just telling me this now?" asked Jack incredulously.

"Because I didn't want you going into Agent Mulder mode and start worrying about me," said Piper.

"You're dating yourself with the *X-Files* thing, and I'm not worried," said Jack. "I just find it really strange, of course, that when there's trouble to be found, you're all over it."

"I don't find it," Piper protested. "It finds *me*."

"Well, I'll make a few calls and let you know if I have anything to report," said Jack. "What's the name?"

"Hart. Shelley Hart."

When they ended their call, Piper checked her Facebook page. She posted the picture of the gorgeous sunset she'd taken earlier with the caption "Just another night in paradise." Afterward she was surprised to find a friend request from Brad O'Hara. She had deliberately avoided him at the dinner party, but obviously he hadn't taken the hint.

Sometimes people she didn't really know tried to "friend her" on Facebook because they had mutual friends. Sometimes, people with no connection at all requested friendship; most were fans who had watched her on *A Little Rain Must Fall*. Piper not so secretly treasured those people. They were always posting comments about how good she was and how much they enjoyed her work. She had gotten into the habit of sharing a few of the details of her continuing quest to land some new gigs. She could actually feel the enthusiasm and affection that her fans had for her as they supported and consoled her. They believed in her even when she herself had doubts.

Since posting the picture of the first wedding cake she'd made for *A Little Rain Must Fall* star Glenna Brooks's marriage on Christmas Eve, and after some of the specifics about the part Piper had played in the capture of another *Little Rain* star's murderer appeared in the press, Piper's Facebook-friend base had grown even larger. She had started to share some of her mother's recipes from The Icing on the Cupcake, the family bakery. That, too, had received a warm welcome, and recently Piper had created an Icing on the Cupcake fan page on Facebook. On both pages Piper took pains to point out that it was her mother who ran the bakery and that Piper was taking on wedding-cake assignments only between acting jobs.

She had just returned from Los Angeles, where last month she'd completed her second wedding cake. The initial contract for a large cake had ended up being substantially downsized when the bride and groom decided they wanted a small and very private ceremony instead of the one they had previously planned. A big wedding seemed inappropriate when death had come to people surrounding the bride.

While Piper was in the City of Angels, her agent, Gabe Leonard, had sent her on an audition for a dog-food commercial. Though she was sure she'd blown the callback audition, she had amazingly gotten the part. Getting that part had been a much-needed morale booster. If it ran often enough, the commercial would also be a welcome boost to her bank account. Her financial situation was embarrassing.

Deciding she would accept Brad O'Hara as a friend on Facebook because he was an actual friend of Kathy and Dan's, Piper clicked on Brad's profile picture, instantly enlarging it as *his* Facebook page came up on the screen. Brad had chosen to post a Fabio-type picture of himself. Suntanned, shirt off, hair tousled as he gazed confidently into the camera.

Piper squinted to get a closer look. Nothing covered the tattoo on his forearm. A woman's face was drawn in dark, indelible ink. Tears fell from the woman's eyes.

Chapter 14

At the last minute, Roz Golubock had called Nora to decline the dinner-party invitation. She was just too tired. Instead she would eat at home by herself.

After supper Roz carefully wrapped the barely touched chicken and stowed it in the refrigerator. She loaded the dishwasher with a single plate, glass, fork, knife, and spoon. She hand-washed the pots that had held the uneaten brown rice and brussels sprouts. Finally, scrubbing the white sink until it sparkled, Roz looked forward to the next day.

Tuesdays she went to the Women's Exchange, where she worked as a volunteer. People consigned or donated their furniture, ceramics, glassware, china, artwork, books, and clothing, which were pounced on by bargain hunters. Profits went to supporting the arts in the form of grants and scholarship programs. To Roz it was a win-win-win. She got to be around beautiful and interesting things, socialize with nice people, and raise money for wonderful causes. She loved it.

Switching off the light in her tiny kitchen, Roz thought she might watch some television before heading up to bed. Though she was very tired, she dreaded climbing the dark stairs by herself. For the last several nights, she'd been restless. Usually a sound sleeper, she kept waking up, listening for any noise.

Before she drew the drapes in the living room, Roz looked out the sliding glass door at the Gulf of Mexico. Lightning zigzagged through the sky. She thought of Sam whenever there was a storm. They used to sit together out on the lanai and wonder at the jagged electric bolts that shattered the darkness. Even when there was no rain or wind onshore, there could be lightning shows out over the Gulf. Tonight, though, there were gusting winds and sheets of rain pounding down.

She could imagine Sam saying, *This one's a beaut, Roz.*

When she and Sam had first bought the town house, they'd been thrilled to get the end unit. They enjoyed their neighbors in the small complex, but they also liked the privacy afforded by being the last one. The long stretch of palm trees, sea grapes, and other tropical foliage that separated the town house from the

Whispering Sands Inn property was like their own private nature preserve.

Weather permitting, they walked the beach every morning and swam in the therapeutic Gulf waters each afternoon. Sam had his golf, and she had her book group and volunteer activities. At the end of the day, they would have their cocktails before dinner and watch the glorious sunsets. Roz missed Sam, missed him deeply, but she knew she was lucky to have had a wonderful marriage for thirty-nine years. She tried to focus on the happiness, not the loss.

It was hard sometimes, though. And since the other night, when she'd seen the man carrying the woman over his shoulders as he disappeared into the foliage, Roz had ached for Sam. He would reassure her. Sam would know what to do.

Roz kept thinking about it. Had the man swept the woman off her feet in a romantic gesture? Had the couple merely been playing? Had the woman been drunk? Or had it been something more sinister and dangerous?

She'd watched and waited, leaving the window only once to go to the bathroom. After a long time, the man finally came out of the foliage again. But he was by himself.

She hadn't been able to see his face but saw him open the trunk of his car and toss in a shovel.

Roz was sure that was what she'd seen.

Chapter 15

*H*e couldn't sleep. He got out of bed and went to the window. His heart raced as he watched the flashes of lightning. The thunderous boom that followed almost immediately signaled that the storm was right on top of them. He prayed it wouldn't last too long.

This was the first storm since he'd buried her. Was the hole deep enough? Could the winds and rain expose the grave? Would the pounding surf rise high enough to wash away the sand?

He'd picked a spot far from the shoreline, up near the vegetation line. There was less traffic there. The morning walkers took their strolls at the water's edge, stopping to pick up seashells and sand dollars washed up on the beach. Sunbathers, too, stayed closer to the water, where they might feel the ocean breeze and easily go for a dip when they got too hot. It seemed that only the sea turtles tried to make it to the vegetation line. The mother sensed that her eggs might have a better chance of survival the farther they were from the seawater that could wash out the nest.

Thankfully, it wasn't turtle nesting season now. It would be several months before the daily turtle patrols began again. For now no volunteers scanned the beach every morning, alert to signs of turtle tracks and mounds of disturbed sand.

As thunder boomed again, he felt his chest tighten. He turned away from the window. There was nothing he could do now. He certainly couldn't fight Mother Nature.

He lay down on the bed and closed his eyes, but his mind continued to race. He wished it had never come to what it had. He wished he hadn't had to kill Shelley, yet he was relieved she was dead. She wasn't going to make any more trouble.

He was pretty certain Levi wasn't going to present a problem. The stricken look on the kid's face almost made him feel sorry for him. And the way Levi had promised not to tell anyone what he'd seen and pleaded for his sister's life had been truly pathetic.

The only other complication was the old lady in the town-house window. What should he do about her?

He soothed himself asleep with the hope that Shelley's body wouldn't be found. Without a body, there was no crime.

Tuesday

A woman's tongue
is the last thing about her that dies.
AMISH PROVERB

Chapter 16

Piper was awakened by a knock on the door. At first she was disoriented, but quickly it came to her: Sarasota and Kathy's wedding. They were going downtown this morning for the dress fittings. She had to get up.

She rolled out of bed and went to the door, opening it a crack. A bellman stood in the hallway holding a tall vase of pink roses.

"For me?" asked Piper, smiling brightly she opened the door wider. "Hold on a minute. Let me get my wallet."

The bellman stepped into the room and set the flowers on the dresser.

Piper pressed a couple of singles into his hand. "Thank you," she said. As soon as the door closed again, she unsealed the small envelope attached to the arrangement.

HAPPY VALENTINE'S DAY, PIPER

LOVE, JACK

She smiled as she studied the card, realizing that it was the first time Jack had actually written the word "love" to her. He had yet to *say* the word. Neither of them had. But Piper had sensed it was coming. She closed her eyes and inhaled the sweet scent of the roses.

She wondered where it would go with Jack. Piper knew he wanted to go further, and in many ways she did, too. But her last foray into love, and the ones before that, had ended with disappointment. Piper was afraid of making another mistake.

Deep in her heart, she acknowledged that love involved taking risks. Being guarded and closed was not the route to happiness. By nature she was open and affectionate. Yet something inside her warned her to be cautious.

Piper laughed out loud at that thought. Her father was always complaining that she was too fearless for her own good, constantly warning her to be careful.

Little do you know, Dad, how careful your little girl can be.

Several of her friends had already gotten married. Now, at twenty-seven, Piper was making wedding cakes, watching more couples pledge to spend their lives together. Were they brave? Did they analyze everything the way she did? Or did they just *know* and merely follow their hearts?

Piper did know one thing: Jack Lombardi was already her best friend.

She walked over to the window and looked outside. It was still raining. Though the lightning and thunder had stopped, the sky was gray and there were whitecaps on the water. She watched a big brown pelican circle before making a clumsy landing on the Gulf. Once settled, the bird floated gracefully, rising and falling with the waves, undeterred by the raindrops.

After a quick shower, Piper started to pull on a pair of jeans but thought better of it. Instead she took her favorite leggings and a light blazer from the closet. She had no idea what Kathy would be wearing this morning or where they'd go for lunch, so she thought it best to dress in something that would be appropriate anywhere.

When she was ready, she proceeded down to the inn's small café, where a continental breakfast was being served. Her parents were already there, lingering over their coffee.

"Hey there, lovey," said Vin when he saw her.

"Happy Valentine's Day, you two," said Piper as she kissed both her parents on the cheek.

"How'd you sleep?" Terri asked.

"I died. Nothing like sleeping to the sound of the ocean."

"The thunder didn't keep you awake?" asked Terri. "It did me."

"Nope," said Piper, pouring herself a bowl of cereal. She took a banana and a container of skim milk from the buffet table.

"I don't think you should leave your windows wide open at night, Piper," said her father. "You're on the ground floor, and anybody could climb right in."

"Okay, Dad," said Piper as she peeled the banana. It was easier to agree than to argue. She was accustomed to her father's preoccupation with safety. Why cause him any more worry than he already had? Piper sometimes wondered what it must be like in her father's mind, always looking three steps down the road to the dire possibilities ready to beset everyone and everything. It exhausted her to think about it.

Terri put down her empty coffee cup. "What time is your appointment for the dress fitting?" she asked.

"Kathy is picking me up at ten," said Piper. "Afterward we're going to go out for lunch, if she's still up for it. What are you guys doing?"

"Nora wants me to come over and look at *her* dress," said Terri. "Then I thought I'd go and buy the ingredients for the cake."

Piper looked concerned. "I could do that with you later this afternoon, Mom," she offered. "Why don't we plan on three o'clock?"

"Great," said Terri. "I'll meet you back here at three."

Piper turned to her father. "What about you, Dad?"

"Dan asked if I wanted to come over to Mote. He's giving a lecture today on sharks and other dangerous sea life."

Piper smirked. "Wow, that's just screaming out your name!"

"Laugh if you want, Piper," said Vin. "But it's always good to know as much as you can about something that could hurt you."

Piper flipped through a magazine as she waited in the lobby for her cousin to arrive. From time to time, she looked toward the entrance. She was surprised to see the young man with whom she'd placed the order for the hex sign at Fisher's gift shop the day before.

He was carrying in a stack of white cardboard bakery boxes. His brow was knit in concentration.

"Hi," said Piper as he got close to her chair.

He stopped and looked at her uncertainly. Piper could tell he didn't immediately recognize her.

"I was in your shop yesterday. I ordered the marriage hex sign?" she reminded him.

The teenager nodded. "Oh, yes. Do not worry. I am going to work on it today."

Piper laughed. "I'm not worried. I didn't expect it to be done that quickly."

She loved to observe people. It helped her as an actress. She never knew when she was going to steal a mannerism she'd noticed and bring it to a character she was playing. She studied the young man's face. His worried expression made her want to reassure him. What was troubling him? She couldn't even speculate. She had no idea what went on in the Amish world.

She gestured to the boxes he was carrying. "Are those pies from Fisher's?" she asked.

"Yes," he said. "I deliver them fresh every morning."

"Yum," said Piper. "My family loves them. It's great to know we don't have to drive all the way over to Pinecraft. We can just have them here. I hope one of those is peanut-butter cream."

The young man smiled a little bit. "Yes, and Dutch apple crumb and southern pecan."

"I'm never going to fit into my bridesmaid's dress," Piper said with a groan. "Whatever. Kathy will have to deal."

Out of the corner of her eye, Piper saw Kathy walking toward them across the lobby. As she drew closer, Piper could see that her cousin's eyes were bloodshot and the skin beneath them was puffy. Either Kathy hadn't slept well or she'd been crying—or maybe both.

"I see you've met Levi," Kathy said.

"Yes . . . well, we haven't actually been formally introduced." Piper stuck out her hand. Levi put the boxes down on the table and returned the handshake. His palms were clammy.

"Nice to meet you," he said politely, immediately picking up the boxes again. "Well, I better get going. I have other deliveries to make."

Piper and her cousin watched as he walked toward the café.

"He's nice," said Piper. "But he seems so serious."

"Levi is a good kid. And so is his sister, Miriam."

"Is she the one who served dinner last night?" asked Piper.

Kathy nodded. "Mm-hmm. She cleans house for Mom and helps some of the other people in the town-house complex. They're both totally honest and such hard workers."

"It must be rough being an Amish teenager," said Piper. "Everyone else their age is out partying and doing things they don't want their parents to find out about."

"Don't worry about Levi, Piper," said Kathy. "He's having fun. He's in the middle of that period when the young people go wild and experience the outside world before they settle down into the Amish life for good. The other night I saw him at the Beach Club, and he was downing those beers like a champ."

Chapter 17

Sitting at his computer and working on the pay-roll, Walter realized that he was in rough shape. Without Shelley to assist him and with Kathy taking time off this week and next for her wedding and honeymoon, he was going to have to do the heavy lifting of managing the inn. That was going to keep him from focusing on his expansion plans.

There was nothing he could do about it. The last thing he'd want to do was deny Kathy the freedom to enjoy this special time in her life. Neither did Walter want to disappoint her mother. Things were going so well between them. He didn't want to do anything that might jeopardize that relationship.

He leaned back in his chair and put his loafer-clad feet up on the desk. All and all, he was content. He really enjoyed the time he spent with her Nora, and the prospect of Kathy as a stepdaughter pleased him greatly. He'd never married or had children of his own, and he'd come to regret it. He'd always been so driven. Now he was trying to have a more balanced life and was finding that he liked it. Sharing meals or catching a movie with Nora, having someone to talk with and care about had enriched his days and nights.

Still, Walter knew himself well enough to realize that he was first, last, and always a businessman. He pulled out the property survey from the drawer, spread it across his desk, and studied it. Each red X marked his progress. It excited him that his persistent attempts to persuade the town-house owners to sell him their property were coming to fruition. He already had six signed contracts. There were four more to sew up before he reached his goal.

The economy was on his side. Across the state there were far too many properties for sale and far too few buyers. Things weren't going to change overnight. Another few weeks wasn't going to alter the real-estate market. He knew he could afford to be patient.

Walter rose from his large desk and walked to the window. He noted with satisfaction that the rain had stopped. Though some was necessary and inevitable, too much rain certainly wasn't good for business.

Suddenly it occurred to him that it was Valentine's Day. He reached for his phone and scrolled through the listings till he came to the florist's number.

"I'd like two dozen red roses delivered to Mrs. Nora Leeds," he said.

It was of utmost importance that he stay in Nora's good graces.

Chapter 18

Kathy walked out of the fitting room. Piper's mouth dropped open and tears welled up in her green eyes.

"You're a goddess!" she gasped. "Kathy, you are *so* beautiful!"

"Do you like it?" asked Kathy.

"Like it? I *love* it!" said Piper.

The dress was strapless, setting off to perfection Kathy's shoulders and décolletage. The bodice was ruched. Beneath it, soft white organza flowed gracefully, creating a slimming A-line silhouette. A sweeping train was attached to the back of the dress.

"Gorgeous," said Piper. "Just gorgeous. But there's one little thing."

Kathy's wide smile disappeared. "What? What's wrong?"

"What about the train?" asked Piper. "You don't want it dragging behind you in the sand, do you?"

Kathy let out a deep sigh. "Of course not," she said, smiling again. "That's where you come in, cuz. You won't mind carrying it for me, will you?"

"Oh, I see. You want me to be your Pippa Middleton," said Piper. "Sure. I'll do anything you want. I just hope my bridesmaid dress makes my butt look as good as hers did."

"Aw, Piper." Kathy laughed as she squeezed her cousin's hand. "Thank you."

"For what?"

"For helping me enjoy this and for taking my mind off Shelley for a little while."

The sun was shining brightly and the sidewalks were already dry when Piper and Kathy came out of the bridal shop.

"Before we go get something to eat, want to stop at the Women's Exchange?" asked Kathy. "There's a mirror I've had my eye on, and I think this is the day that the price reduces. That is, if it's still there."

"Great," said Piper. "I love that place. I'll look in the book section to find something to read while I'm here."

The long, low building was covered in pink stucco. The parking lot in front was full, and they had to wait for a space to open up. They watched from the car as workmen unloaded a truckful of furniture.

"I hardly buy anything new anymore," said Kathy. "I always check here first. Sooner or later I usually find just what I want, or something even better than I had in mind. It's saving Dan and me a ton of money while we're setting up our place."

When they got inside, Kathy steered Piper through the other shoppers to the rear of the store. "What do you think?" she asked, pointing to the mirror hanging on the wall.

Piper considered it. "I like the shape. Is the frame hand-painted?"

Kathy nodded as she checked the price tag. "I could wait a few weeks and the price would come down even more," she said. "But I don't want to take the chance that somebody else will buy it."

"Go for it," said Piper.

Kathy gestured for one of the male workers to take the mirror down.

"It will be up at the front desk when you're ready to check out," he said.

They wandered through the aisles. While Kathy browsed in the china-and-glassware section, Piper selected Tina Fey's autobiography and two paperback novels from the shelves at the other side of the store. She spotted a necklace she admired in the jewelry department.

"Would you like to try it on?" asked the white-haired woman behind the counter.

"Yes. Thank you," said Piper.

"It looks good on you," said the woman as Piper fastened the strand around her neck. "The turquoise brings out the green of your eyes."

As Piper observed herself in the mirror, Kathy walked up beside her.

"Hi, Mrs. Golubock!" she said, recognizing her mother's neighbor. "I forgot that you work here on Tuesdays."

"Hello, Kathy." The older woman smiled. "Nice to see you. How are the wedding plans coming?"

"They're coming," said Kathy. "In fact, this is my cousin Piper, my maid of honor. She just came down from New Jersey yesterday."

"Nice to meet you, Piper," said Mrs. Golubock. Piper shook the frail, manicured hand the woman offered.

Golubock. Golubock. Piper tried to remember where she'd heard the name. Last night at dinner. This was the woman who'd seen a man carrying what she thought was a woman's body into the vegetation near the condo.

Piper looked at Kathy and waited for her cousin to bring up the subject. But Kathy steered the conversation to the wedding and her hopes that the weather would be good on Saturday.

Finally Piper took off the necklace. "I'm going to think about it," she said, ever conscious of her tight budget.

As Piper returned the necklace to Mrs. Golubock, the woman closed her eyes, wobbled forward, and collapsed to the floor.

Chapter 19

Dr. Robbins pulled the last sheet off the prescription pad. As usual, he'd been going through them quickly this morning. Some were for patients he'd had for a long time, and some were for recent referrals. It was gratifying to see how word spread when patients were satisfied.

He opened his desk drawer, looking for another pad. Finding none, Dr. Robbins immediately picked up the phone to call out to the reception desk.

"Umiko, I'm out of scrips," he said in exasperation. "You have to order some more, fast."

"I'll be right there, Cryder dear," answered Umiko.

Almost instantly there was a soft knock, and then the doctor's door opened. Umiko stood there smiling, holding up a small blue pad in one hand and a box of chocolates in the other. "How could you think I would ever let you run out?" she asked coyly. "I've ordered more."

His frown morphed into a smile as he remembered the Japanese custom on Valentine's Day. The woman gave the man candy. Next month, on March 14, "White Day," Cryder would reciprocate with a gift of his own. He had a jade bracelet in mind. "I should have known better," he said, taking the pad and candy from his wife. He put the new prescription pad in the desk drawer.

"Don't forget to lock it," said Umiko. "We don't want someone ripping us off again. Those scrips are too tempting a prize for some of our patients. They'd rather have those than one of your precious netsuke."

"You don't have to remind me, Umiko." He nodded at the door. "How many more are out there?" he asked.

"Four."

"So many?"

Umiko leaned down and kissed him on the forehead. "That's what you get for having so many satisfied customers."

Dr. Robbins sighed. "They're patients, Umiko, not customers. I hate it when you call them customers."

"Sorry, dear. You're right, of course."

Umiko turned to go back out to the reception area, then stopped and pivoted around.

"Cryder?"

"Hmm?" He was straightening the line of small ivory figures on his desk.

"You haven't changed your mind, have you?"

"About what?" he asked absentmindedly.

"About selling our place to Walter Engel for the Whispering Sands expansion."

Cryder's head shot up. "Absolutely not! First of all, because I know you don't want to sell, and second, because I don't want to sell to *him*. I don't like the way he conducts business."

Chapter 20

Going over the table-arrangement chart for the wedding breakfast on Saturday, Isaac thought about Kathy Leeds and how sorry he was that this whole business with Shelley was upsetting her right before the wedding. He couldn't say that *he* had missed not having Shelley around for the last few days. Her absence made his life so much easier.

Though Walter Engel owned the Whispering Sands Inn, Isaac had little contact with him. Shelley was his supervisor. She oversaw all the events held at the hotel. If clients wanted a wedding reception, family reunion, business meeting, or some other kind of organized gathering, they booked it with Shelley. It was Isaac's responsibility to draw up plans for the events and implement them.

He treasured his job. Isaac loved coming up with an artistic vision and bringing things together. His concepts were always big and lush—in direct opposition to the simple, plain way he was brought up. Isaac liked things lavish and unrestrained. He believed that if you wanted something special, you just had to be willing to pay for it. That's the way it was.

Shelley was far more concerned with the bottom line. That was where they always came to professional loggerheads. Shelley offered the client an estimate, and Isaac had to bring the event in under that amount in order for the hotel to make a profit. He did his best, often required to put aside his own creative vision in favor of doing something less expensively. Still, Shelley was forever shooting down his ideas as being too grand and too costly. She was always keeping him from doing what he really wanted.

Though Isaac had stood up for himself in his disagreements with her, Shelley had the final say. If he wanted to keep his job, he had to kowtow to her wishes. He scaled back his plans and tried hard to get more bang for the buck. It had become increasingly frustrating, but he'd found a way to compensate himself for her aggravation.

It started with the mosaic of the sea turtles. He had long admired its beauty and artistry. But its size and prominence had been a challenge. Isaac had disarmed the security cameras and learned the night watchman's routine. Pulling off the theft was quite an accomplishment.

His mistake was in getting sick for a week. Unannounced, Shelley had come to the apartment to drop off his paycheck. Elliott, unaware that the mosaic hanging over the sofa was stolen, let Shelley in. She looked around and left without saying a word.

When Isaac returned to work, Shelley confronted him, outraged by his dishonesty. He begged her not to tell Walter or the police, and to give him another chance.

Isaac had already been looking for another job just in case. The Sarasota Ritz-Carlton and the Hyatt had event planners who weren't going anywhere. Besides, he had no real desire to relocate.

As he made a note to himself to add a small round table for Kathy's wedding cake, Isaac knew that without Shelley he could stay right here at the Whispering Sands Inn. Life would be so much easier.

Chapter 21

Piper and Kathy ran behind the counter to help.

"Mrs. Golubock! Roz!" Kathy leaned over the older woman and took hold of her hand. "Are you all right?"

Roz's eyes were closed, and all color had drained from her face. Blood oozed from a cut on her forehead. But her chest moved up and down: She was breathing.

"She really slammed her head against the edge of the counter on the way down," said Piper. "Someone call 911!" she shouted to no one in particular.

"I'll do it!" yelled one of the other exchange volunteers.

Customers quickly crowded around, craning their necks to see what had happened. Kathy knelt beside Roz, rubbing her hand. Piper tried to remember the first aid her father had taught her. Roz had fainted, which meant that the blood supply to her brain was momentarily inadequate, causing her to temporarily lose consciousness. At least that's what Piper suspected.

"Somebody get me something to prop up her legs," Piper commanded. "Kathy, can you loosen her belt? And is there a first-aid kit around here?"

A low stool from the display floor was handed across the counter. Piper lifted Roz's legs above heart level. Kathy opened the first-aid kit that was thrust at her.

"Take one of those gauze pads and apply some pressure," said Piper. "Head cuts bleed a lot. Hopefully it's not as bad as it looks."

When Roz opened her eyes, Piper breathed a sigh of guarded relief. The woman tried to raise herself.

"Don't get up too quickly, Mrs. Golubock," said Piper. "Just rest a few minutes."

Roz was sitting up when the paramedics arrived. They checked her vital signs and treated the cut. When the blood was wiped away, the abrasion turned out to be relatively minor.

"Let's take a ride to the emergency room and have a doc check you out," said the paramedic.

"I'm telling you I'm fine," Roz insisted. "Though I admit that I'm stupid. I didn't eat any breakfast this morning. I'm so sorry to have bothered everyone like this."

After another unsuccessful attempt to persuade Roz to go to the hospital, the paramedic had her sign a document stating that she had denied the offer of further medical treatment.

"At least you have to get someone to take you home," said the paramedic. "You shouldn't be driving."

"We'll take her," said Kathy. "Roz can go with me, and Piper can drive her car home."

"All right," said the paramedic as his partner packed up the emergency gear. "But remember: Fainting can have no big medical significance or it can be the sign of something more serious. You should have yourself checked out by your own physician."

Chapter 22

Walking to the water's edge, Brad stuck his bare foot into the now-calm waters of the Gulf. Very cool, but not truly cold. He looked up at the sky. The sun was shining brightly.

The morning had been dead, but Brad had hopes that the afternoon would improve. It was the season, after all, and the snowbirds would be desperate to get to the beach. Kayaks and paddleboards provided the chance for exercise as well as a suntan.

He liked having the beach to himself, but he was relieved when he saw people begin straggling onto the stretch of white sand. They carried their towels and chairs and umbrellas, willing to lug all that paraphernalia for the opportunity to soak up some rays.

He wondered if Piper Donovan would be coming out to sun herself this afternoon. That white skin of hers could use a little color. He'd love to see Piper in a bikini. She might even look better in one than Shelley had.

Chapter 23

Piper and Kathy escorted Mrs. Golubock into her town house. Roz held on to the wrought-iron railing as she walked slowly down the few steps that led to the living room. She lowered herself gingerly into the rocker by the sliding-glass door.

"Maybe we should give your daughter a call and tell her what happened," suggested Kathy.

"Oh, no. I don't want to bother Roberta. She'll want to get on a plane and fly right down here. I'm absolutely fine. Really I am."

"How about we get you something to eat?" asked Piper. "I can run down to Anna's Deli. What kind of sandwich would you like?"

Roz shook her head as she gazed out at the water. "No thank you, Piper," she said. "I have plenty of food in the kitchen. I just have to make sure to eat it. I haven't had much of an appetite for the last few days."

"I think that paramedic is right, Roz," said Kathy. "You should see a doctor." She pulled out her cell phone. "I'm going to call Dr. Robbins."

"I had a checkup just last month," Roz murmured. "There's nothing wrong with me. Nothing physical anyway."

"Well, what *is* bothering you?" Piper asked gently. "Maybe there's something we can do to help."

Roz looked at each of them and realized that it would be a relief to relate what she had seen the other night.

"Would you stay and have a cup of tea with me?" asked Roz. "I'll tell you what's on my mind."

Chapter 24

They learned their lesson the hard way. The giant sand castle they'd spent hours building the day before was completely gone. The seashell-studded turrets and deep moat had been washed away by the wind, rain, and surf.

"Guys, let's build another one—a better one," said the sunburned college kid on midterm break. "But not so close to the water this time."

The four fraternity brothers carried their towels and the plastic ice buckets they'd pilfered from their hotel rooms up the beach. They stopped at an area near the vegetation line.

"This looks like a good place. And the sand is still moist. Great for packing."

"Let's make it twice as big as the one we made yesterday, and let's get really into it with the decorations.

You guys start digging, and I'll search around for some cool shells and stuff."

"Why do *we* have to do all the manual labor?"

"Bro, you're an idiot. You go search for shells, and I'll stay here with these guys and get the important stuff done."

Within an hour they had molded dozens of sand blocks and stacked them in towers of varying heights. One of the boys went down to the shoreline, filled his bucket with water, and blended it with sand. He drizzled the mixture on the tops of the towers to form tall Gothic spires.

"Hey, dudes, I found a load of shark teeth," called the one who had gone in search of decorations as he returned. "They'll be wicked on top of the castle wall, like spikes to keep out the barbarians."

When they were finished, they stood back to observe their handiwork and marvel at the architectural triumph.

"I gotta go get my iPhone," said one. "I wanna take a picture of this."

"Wait! We're not done yet. We have to dig the moat."

Chapter 25

"I can see why you'd be worried," said Piper, pretending she hadn't heard the story at dinner the night before. "I'd be terrified, too, if I saw somebody going into the bushes with a body slung over his shoulder."

"It's probably too late now," said Roz, putting down her teacup. "I should have called the minute I saw it. But I didn't want to trouble the sheriff's deputies again."

"Again?" asked Piper.

"Well, I've called them several times about one thing or another since my Sam died. I could tell the last time that the officer was just humoring me."

"It's their *job* to help," said Piper.

"Let's call right now," said Kathy. "They should know if someone is prowling around here. And, God forbid, what if what you saw had something to do with my friend Shelley's disappearance?"

Chapter 26

A murderous creature loomed ferociously from the screen in the Mote Marine Aquarium lecture hall. The marine biologist at the front of the room continued with his presentation on some of the most dangerous sea life in the world.

"This is a tiger shark," explained Dan Clemens. "It's a savage predator capable of devouring fish, seals, other sharks, and even birds flying *above* the water. It has powerful jaws that can easily crush a sea turtle or other marine mammal."

Dan directed his laser pointer at the shark's eyes. "Tiger sharks have excellent vision and sense of smell, which allow them to locate a drop of blood in an area the size of a football field."

A white-haired man in the front row raised his hand. "Are there tiger sharks around here?"

"This tiger shark was found near the Central Pacific islands," said Dan. "But make no mistake, there are various shark species in the Gulf of Mexico. And while sharks usually avoid human beings and attacks are exceedingly rare, there are things you should do to further lessen the chance. On your way out today, pick up one of our free pamphlets on the subject."

Dan continued with the show. Sea snakes could paralyze their enemies. Moray eels possessed teeth designed to tear flesh. Stingrays hid under the sand on the ocean floor before shooting their prey with poison. A blue-ringed octopus was strangely beautiful but carried enough venom to kill twenty-six people. Pufferfish toxins were more powerful than cyanide.

"The toxins paralyze the victim. It's not a pretty picture. Sweating, headaches, tremors, seizures, cardiac arrhythmias, and respiratory failure. Although completely paralyzed, the victim may be conscious and lucid before death, able to see and hear but unable to speak or move. It's a horrible way to die."

Vin's hand shot up again. "Is there any treatment?"

"No antidote has been approved for human use yet," said Dan. "Treatment usually involves pumping out the stomach and taking standard life-support measures to keep the victim alive until the effects of the poison wear off. Not everyone dies. *If* the patient survives twenty-four hours, he'll usually live. But that's a very big if."

Chapter 27

A flash of scarlet caught their eyes. They dug farther, recoiling in horror when they saw what it was. The bright red was painted on a human toenail. Openmouthed, the fraternity brothers drew closer together and stared into the trench.

"What the . . . ?"

"No way!"

One of them reached down, cautiously pushing away more sand, revealing the rest of the foot. A delicate gold bracelet encircled a thin ankle. He recoiled and dropped his plastic bucket.

"We can't dig anymore," he commanded. "We gotta call the cops."

Chapter 28

While she and Kathy waited with Roz for the deputy from the sheriff's department to arrive, Piper took the plates and teacups into the kitchen. As she was rinsing them, she glanced up and looked out the window over the sink. Three law-enforcement vehicles came careening down the driveway, emergency lights flashing.

"They're here already," Piper called to Roz and Kathy. "But I can't believe they've sent three cars."

The white sedans came to a stop in front of Roz's unit. The deputies got out and hurried right past the town house, running into the vegetation at the side of the property. Piper quickly dried her hands and returned to the living room.

"They aren't here for us," she said. "I'm going out to see what's happening."

————

Piper joined the small crowd that had gathered on the beach, watching as officers cordoned off an area of sand and foliage with stakes and yellow tape. She noticed Brad O'Hara standing on the periphery of the group. He was shirtless despite the cool breeze. Piper went over to talk to him, getting a clear view of the crying woman's face tattooed on his arm.

"What happened?" she asked.

"Some kids found a body," he answered flatly, his eyes glued to the crime scene.

Standing on tiptoe and craning her neck, Piper watched as the officers shoveled, carefully placing the sand they dug up into piles. Two men dressed in street clothes crouched at the edge of the pit looking down into it, while another took photographs.

"Okay, everybody. Stand back," ordered one of the deputies. "Stand back!"

The spectators obeyed, but just barely. Piper separated herself from the crowd and then inconspicuously made her way to a spot where she could get a better view. She noticed that Brad had followed her.

"Oh, dear God!" cried an onlooker as the sand-covered body was lifted from the hole. The dead woman's eyes were closed. Her skin was gray, and her matted dark hair hung long and loose. She was dressed in a short skirt and a yellow cotton sweater, which stretched tightly across her chest. Her feet were bare, and her arms were stiff. Piper noticed there were several rings on her fingers and a small tattoo on her left hand in the space between the thumb and forefinger. Piper couldn't make out the design. She was trying to identify the mark when Brad O'Hara stepped forward.

"I know who she is," he said. "Her name is Shelley Hart."

Piper stood by and was able to listen while one of the officers questioned Brad.

"I've known Shelley since we were at Sarasota High together," Brad said. "We hung out. In fact, I was with her when she got that little cupid tattoo on her hand." He hesitated for a moment before continuing. "I might as well tell you—if you ask around, you'll find out—I've done a stretch in jail."

"For what?" asked the deputy.

"Dealing," answered Brad. "But that was years ago—I'm totally legit now. You can confirm all that."

The deputy showed no reaction. "When had you seen Ms. Hart last?" he asked.

"Last week," said Brad. "She came over to the pavilion where I run my business. She wanted to make sure that I had enough kayaks for a wedding group that would be staying at the inn."

"When exactly was that?"

Brad thought back and calculated. "I think it was last Tuesday."

"Did you notice anything out of the ordinary?" asked the deputy. "Did she seem upset or worried about anything?"

Brad shook his head. "No, she seemed like Shelley."

"Which means what?" asked the deputy.

"Look, she didn't stay long or talk to me about much. Shelley spoke to me only if she absolutely had to. After I went to prison, she pretty much washed her hands of me."

Piper took out her phone and snapped a picture. Distasteful as it was, a photo of a crime scene would get lots of comments from her Facebook friends.

Chapter 29

Walter's heart sank as he stood at his office window and watched the people striding past the inn on their way up the beach. Word had spread quickly. Everyone was curious about the unearthing of a dead body. They wanted to see the site and be able to tell their friends.

Surely there would be stories on the news tonight and in the newspaper tomorrow morning. While interest in both the event and the investigation would be high in the short run, Walter worried about the long-term effect of the discovery. Would it ultimately be bad for business? Would people recoil from staying at a place so closely associated with something so horrible?

The phone rang. Walter turned away from the window, went to his desk, and picked up the receiver.

The woman identified herself as a reporter with the local television station.

"Mr. Engel, I'm hoping you would be willing to do a short interview with us about the woman found buried on the beach at the end of the Whispering Sands property. I've just about finished shooting at the scene and could be over to your office within half an hour."

Calculating, Walter quickly decided it would be better to accept the request. He could take the opportunity to declare how shocked and saddened everyone at the inn was and simultaneously give reassurances that the Whispering Sands Inn was a safe and totally reputable establishment. What was that saying? *Any publicity is good publicity.* If he declined, it could look as if he had something to hide.

Walter was waiting in the lobby to greet the reporter. She carried a black equipment bag and a tripod over her shoulder.

"Where's your crew?" he asked, glancing behind her.

The reporter laughed. "There is no crew. Only me."

Walter looked at her quizzically.

"Budget cuts and advanced technology," she said. "I shoot the pictures, conduct the interviews, write the story, and edit the piece all by my little ol' self." She glanced at her watch. "Shall we get started?"

The reporter surveyed the room and decided that the area was too dark. With time at a premium, she didn't want to bother setting up extra lighting and suggested they go outside instead. Walter led the way.

"How about here?" he asked. "With the Gulf in the background."

She set up her tripod and attached the camera to it. When she had it positioned properly and had fastened a microphone to Walter's shirt, she announced she was ready to go.

"I'll stand behind the camera and ask you questions," she said. "Ready?"

Walter took a deep breath and nodded.

"Mr. Engel, the body hasn't been formally identified, but a man on the beach said he recognized the young woman. He wouldn't appear on camera, but he said she's Shelley Hart and she worked here at the Whispering Sands Inn."

Swallowing hard, Walter paused for a few minutes before answering. "Until there is a formal identification, I wouldn't want to comment on that," he said.

"What was Shelley Hart's job here?" asked the reporter.

"I'm sorry, but I don't think it's appropriate to comment."

"Why not?" asked the reporter. "What does it hurt to disclose the dead woman's employment?"

"Because Shelley Hart has not been identified. Until that time comes, Ms. Lehane, I'm not going to talk about her."

The reporter shrugged and took another tack. "All right. What do you think about a dead body being discovered on your property? We can agree to that much, can't we?"

"Of course. This is a terrible thing, a tragic thing. It's especially upsetting since it's so close to home. Unfortunately, things like this happen too much in our society. It could happen anywhere."

"One more question, Mr. Engel. Do you have an opinion as to who might have wanted to kill Shelley Hart?"

Damn this woman. She just won't give up, will she?

Walter hesitated before sputtering out his answer. "Shelley is the kind of woman . . . I mean, she wasn't the kind of woman . . ." He stopped to compose himself before completing his comment. "*If* it is Shelley—and that's a very big if—I don't know the answer to your question. I can't imagine who would want her dead."

Chapter 30

When Piper returned to Roz Golubock's town house, the elderly woman was sitting with a blood-pressure cuff on her arm and her legs up on the sofa. Kathy was frowning.

"It's a little low, Roz," she said, unwrapping the cuff. "You've got to be more diligent about taking your medication."

"I know," said Roz. "I just forget sometimes."

"Well, hang a calendar on your fridge or somewhere. Mark it off every time you take it. You've got to keep track, Roz. This time you're okay, but the next time you might really hurt yourself."

Dreading what she knew she had to tell Kathy, Piper looked at her cousin with admiration. "I'm impressed," said Piper. "I can't believe you actually know how to read that thing."

"I had a lot of practice with my father," said Kathy matter-of-factly. "I want to be able to tell Dr. Robbins and see what he says."

Kathy made the call, relayed the blood-pressure figures and listened.

"Okay, ten o'clock," she said. "We'll make sure that she's there." Kathy ended the call and turned to Roz. "He said he'd feel better if you came in tomorrow morning to see him."

With that settled, Kathy suddenly remembered. "Hey, what was happening out there on the beach, Piper?"

Chapter 31

Levi sat in the gift shop, trying to keep his attention focused on the large white wooden disk on the worktable in front of him. He had carefully sketched out the figures around the periphery of the circle. Now he would begin painting them.

His hand shook as he picked up the brush and dipped it in the red paint. As he brought the brush to the wood, a droplet dribbled beyond the lines that defined the first bird. Levi wiped at the paint with a cloth, only spreading the stain. Now he would have to sand and re-cover the spot with white paint and wait for it to dry before he could continue.

He was determined to get the hex sign finished. He had given his word to Piper Donovan, and he wanted Kathy and Dan to have something to remember him by. He wanted to make sure that it would be meaningful.

Levi blew on the wet paint, willing it to dry faster. He felt pressured and scared.

He couldn't find his cell phone. He'd looked for it everywhere. He'd retraced his steps, returning to the Whispering Sands Inn, hoping he had put it down in the kitchen when he'd delivered the pies this morning. He'd searched the lobby area, beneath cushions and under the chairs. He'd checked with the receptionist, but nobody had turned it in.

Levi followed the exact same path all the way back to Pinecraft. He carefully scanned the trail, searching in vain, feeling more and more desperate. The last time he remembered using the cell phone was the previous night. Right before he went to Shelley's grave.

Chapter 32

After breaking the news of the discovery of Shelley's body, Piper wrapped her arm around her cousin's shoulders as they walked back to her mother's town house.

"I can't believe it! I just can't believe that Shelley is dead!" Kathy cried. "How can this be happening?"

Pulling her cousin closer, Piper whispered, "I don't know, Kathy. I'm sorry. I'm so sorry."

They traveled the rest of the way in a silence punctuated only by the sound of the driveway pebbles crunching beneath their feet and Kathy's weeping. When they got to the front door, Kathy paused.

"Wait a minute," she said, opening her purse and pulling out a tissue. "Let me clean myself up. There are only four days before the wedding, and I don't want my mother to see me so upset."

Zipper, the black-and-white cat, was waiting at the front door, but Nora and Terri barely looked up when Piper and Kathy walked into the town house. Their eyes were riveted to the television screen. The twenty-four-hour local news channel was reporting on the grisly discovery. A female reporter told the story.

"A woman's body was found on the beach on the northern part of Siesta Key today. College students vacationing in Sarasota on semester break found the body as they built a sand castle."

A shirtless, unshaven young man appeared on the screen and spoke. *"Man, when I saw that foot sticking out of the sand, it totally freaked me out."*

"While beach lovers looked on, police secured the crime scene and searched for clues."

"It didn't appear like she'd been there too long," said a sheriff's deputy. *"There was no noticeable decomposition."*

"The burial site was on the far end of the property of Whispering Sands Inn. The owner was clearly shaken."

"Look, there's Walter!" cried Nora as she pointed at the screen. Walter looked uncomfortable as he squinted against the sun and commented.

"Of course, this a terrible thing, a tragic thing. It's especially upsetting since it's so close to home.

Unfortunately, things like this happen too much in our society. It could happen anywhere."

The reporter appeared again.

"The body of the woman was taken to the Sarasota Memorial Hospital morgue, where an autopsy will be performed. Her identity is being withheld until next of kin can be notified. Lois Ryan for Peninsula News, on Siesta Key."

"Awful," said Nora as she clicked off the set.

"It gets worse, Mom," Kathy said quietly.

Nora looked at her daughter and noticed her red-rimmed eyes. "What?" she asked with urgency. "What's wrong?"

Kathy sat down next to her mother on the sofa and took her hand. "It was Shelley."

Chapter 33

After the body was taken away and the onlookers drifted off, sheriff's deputies continued to search the area. Scanning the beach was a relatively simple matter. The sun shone brightly, illuminating the smooth white sand. Metal detectors led the way to a safety pin, a hair clip, and some bottle caps.

"I doubt these have anything to do with anything," said a deputy as he put the items into plastic evidence bags.

"You never know," said his partner.

Searching the vegetation area took more time. The leather ferns and sea grapes that covered the ground were heavily shaded by taller elderberry, Australian pine, and palm trees. The lack of light and the density of ground growth made the hunt for evidence more difficult.

The deputy picked up a ripped rubber flip-flop and held it out.

"It's so faded," observed the other. "It looks like it's been out here a long time. But bag it anyway."

The deputy squatted down at the base of a palm tree where the weathered shell of a baby sea turtle lay in the sand. "The little guy didn't make it last season," he said ruefully.

"Over here," called the other deputy. "I found something."

In his glove-covered hand, he held up a cell phone.

Chapter 34

*T*hey found her. They found Shelley. It was on television, on the radio, and it would be splashed across the front page of the newspaper in the morning.

Sarasota was a city, but in some ways it was like a small town. This wasn't New York or Chicago or Los Angeles, where the discovery of a dead body could go virtually unnoticed. In Sarasota, uncovering Shelley Hart's body was huge news, especially because she'd been found on Siesta Beach. Everybody paid attention.

Sarasota's financial system revolved around the tourist trade. Visitors pumped millions of dollars into the local economy. The designation of Siesta Beach as the best beach in the nation had been a tremendous boon to hotels, restaurants, theaters, boat- and car-rental companies, and all the other enterprises that provided what *tourists wanted. As a result, the district tax coffers had benefited immensely.*

The image of the perfect spot for vacationers didn't include a dead body in the soft white sand. The police would be under enormous pressure to solve this one. The city needed to be able to reassure everyone that law enforcement was on the ball and that Sarasota was a safe place.

It wouldn't take long for them to get around to interviewing the old gal. Maybe she hadn't actually seen anything that would be incriminating. But maybe she had.

Chapter 35

Kathy insisted that her guests go ahead with the Valentine's Day plans to see *Soul Crooners*. She was too upset and wanted to stay in with Dan for the night. So Piper, her parents, and Nora went to the show.

"Walter wanted to come," said Nora as they drove downtown, "but he just had too much work to do. He feels terrible about Shelley, but he's also concerned about her workload and how he's going to get that covered. Plus, he's worried about how all this is going to impact business at the inn."

"My bet is that it won't hurt business at all," said Vin. "He's got some prime real estate there, with first-class accommodations and some of the best views in the world. People are still going to want to stay at Whispering Sands."

"I second that emotion," said Piper from the back-seat, thinking about the Westcoast Black Theatre Troupe performance they were about to see. She was looking forward to a couple of hours of feel-good music. She wanted to erase the image of Shelley's sand-covered body from her mind.

They found seats in the second row to the right of the stage and began perusing the program. Piper scanned the list of songs that would be sung and the bios of the performers. She was reminded again of how many actors, singers, and other entertainers were out there, plugging away, taking whatever roles they could get, attempting to piece together a living doing what they loved. Just like her.

Piper watched as the all-male group of performers bounded out onto the stage in their white suits and purple shirts. They immediately began singing and dancing to Stevie Wonder's "Signed, Sealed, Delivered I'm Yours." As Piper's foot tapped to the rhythm of the music, her mind kept wandering to the scene on the beach that day.

Why would anyone want to kill Shelley? Had she been deliberately murdered? Or had someone wanted to cover up her accidental death? And what about Brad O'Hara? Could he be connected in some way? He'd admitted that Shelley didn't want to have anything to do with him. Why?

By the time the crooners were singing "My Girl," Piper was wondering about the time immediately before Shelley's death. What had it been like for her? Had she been filled with terror? Or had she not even seen it coming?

The ensemble kept up their nonstop show, performing one unforgettable Motown melody after another. Their enthusiasm was contagious. Some in the audience rose to their feet and danced in place, while others smiled broadly, rocking with the beat in their seats. Piper tried unsuccessfully to focus on the music.

It was unlikely that the burial spot had been picked at random. Somebody was familiar with that place. Was it the man Roz Golubock saw?

As Marvin Gaye's "What's Going On" wrapped up, Piper thought about Brad O'Hara. She was curious about his relationship with Shelley. She could ask Dan, but she also was wondering why the groom-to-be had such a seemingly sketchy friend.

Chapter 36

It was getting increasingly difficult to drive at night. But for as long as she was able, Roz was going to continue to go to her book-club meetings. She enjoyed the book selections and the lively, thoughtful discussions. Roz also took pleasure in the fact that she was by far the oldest club member.

Listening to the younger people expressing their views was invigorating to Roz. They got her to look at things in other ways. And they in turn treated her with respect and valued her opinions. Roz knew she'd eventually have to make the switch and find a club that met in the afternoons. She feared that another club wouldn't be as good, that other members would all be too elderly.

As she backed out of the drive, Roz hoped that none of her neighbors were looking out their town-house windows. Word traveled quickly in the condo development, and she knew that nobody would approve of her going out when she had fainted just that morning. But she felt much better. What was the point of staying in all by herself tonight when she could go out and be with people?

Additionally, knowing that the young woman had been found dead so close to her town house, Roz wanted to get out and be among the living. She didn't want to sit in and dwell on the knowledge that the detectives were coming to interview her in the morning. She felt slightly guilty that she had put them off when they called, wanting to come see her tonight. She had fibbed, saying that she didn't feel up to it, when it was really that she didn't want to miss her book-club meeting.

Roz slowly coasted down the driveway. As she turned out onto Ocean Boulevard, she had no inkling that not only was someone watching her, he was following her.

Chapter 37

On the way home, they raved about the show.

"Did you see how those guys moved?" asked Vin. "Unbelievable."

"And the songs were the sound track of our school years," said Terri. "I can remember dancing to them at fraternity parties."

"Frank and I picked 'La-La Means I Love You' for our first dance at our wedding," said Nora. "I was thinking of him tonight. I so wish he could be here for Kathy and Dan's wedding."

"He will be," said Terri, taking her sister-in-law's hand. "He'll be watching the whole thing."

Piper was about to offer her opinion as the car turned onto Siesta Drive, heading to the North Bridge, which led back to the key. Ahead of them a long string of bright red taillights lined up, reaching all the way to the drawbridge. Vin slowed the car.

"There's no construction going on, and they don't open the bridge for boats to pass through at night," Nora said anxiously as she stretched to get a better view. "I hope there wasn't an accident."

Vin shifted the car into park and turned off the ignition. For fifteen minutes they waited. Finally they saw flashing blue lights heading toward them.

"Oh, no," said Terri as an emergency vehicle sped past. "Seeing an ambulance makes me shiver. I hope it isn't too serious."

Slowly the traffic began to move. Their car followed the others up and over the drawbridge. At the other side, they slowed again as red flares and police lights illuminated the area at the foot of the bridge.

"Rubberneckers," Vin said with disgust. "Everybody's got to get a look at what happened."

At the side of the road, a badly mangled yellow convertible was on its side. The windshield was a spiderweb of cracks. The front door was lying on the ground a few yards away.

Vin whistled through his teeth. "Uh-oh," he said. "It looks like they had to use the Jaws of Life to get out whoever was in there."

"Oh, no!" cried Nora. "I think that's Roz Golubock's car!"

Vin pulled to the side of the road and parked. "You all wait here," he ordered as he opened the door. "I'll find out what happened."

Piper ignored her father's command, got out, and followed him. As they walked toward one of the sheriff's deputies, Piper noticed that long black skid marks streaked across the road. She listened as her father identified himself as a former New York City cop. The two men shook hands.

"It looks like somebody deliberately ran the woman off the road," said the deputy. "We have a witness, a guy who was fishing off the bridge, who says he heard brakes squeal and the sound of a collision. Apparently a car just rammed into the convertible and kept on going. But the witness didn't get the tag and only describes the car as dark. A lot of good that does us."

"And the driver of the convertible?" asked Vin.

"An old woman," said the deputy.

"Was her name Golubock?" asked Vin.

"As a matter of fact, it was. You know her?"

"She's a neighbor of my sister-in-law's," said Vin. He warily eyed the crushed and twisted metal. "Did she make it?"

"So far," said the deputy. "The ambulance took her to Sarasota Memorial. When she left here, she was still conscious. Incoherent but conscious."

Chapter 38

Brad stood in the shower with his eyes closed, letting the needles of hot spray douse him. It felt good to wash away the tension that gripped his muscles. It had been a hard day.

Seeing Shelley's body had brought back so many memories. They'd had a good thing going once, but her brother's death had changed all that. After Colin overdosed on the drugs that Brad had sold him, Shelley had freaked and turned on him. Her testimony had been instrumental in sending Brad to prison.

He picked up the soap and began lathering his body. He rubbed the bar over his forearm and watched as bubbles scattered across his tattoo. The outline of the woman's face and the tears dripping down her cheeks were dark and distinct—surprising, since the ink had been improvised, using melted rubber from the sole of a shoe.

Tattooing was forbidden in the prison. It was done in secret with makeshift equipment. Staples and paper clips took the place of sterilized needles. Ink could be taken from pens or made using melted plastic or Styrofoam. The risk of infection was great. The risk of getting caught and being sent to solitary confinement for a couple of weeks for giving or receiving a tattoo was even greater. This heightened the thrill.

Brad had studied the classic prison tattoos and their meanings. The clock face without hands signified doing time. Tombstones with numbers on them signified the number of years in jail. The letters SWP stood for "supreme white power." And 100% PURE was another "white pride" tattoo.

The face of the crying woman meant that the prisoner had a devoted female on the outside waiting for his release. Brad chose that one but had his own interpretation for it. His woman wasn't crying as she waited for him. His woman was *going* to cry when he got out. Brad had vowed that he was going to make Shelley cry when he saw her again. He was going to make her pay.

Chapter 39

Piper, her parents, and Nora sat in the ER waiting room. They looked up every time the door opened, straining to see into the treatment room. Eventually Dr. Robbins came out to speak with them.

"Thankfully Roz is alive, but she's delirious," he said. "She's pretty banged up."

"How serious are her injuries, Cryder?" asked Nora.

"At Roz's age any injury can be a serious one," said the doctor, unwrapping the stethoscope from around his neck. "We're going to keep her here for observation. We want to make sure she's not bleeding internally and doesn't have a head injury. I don't like that she's so confused. We'll run some tests in the morning."

"Did she say anything about what happened?" asked Piper.

"Not really," said Dr. Robbins. "But she keeps asking for Sam."

"Poor thing," said Nora. "I should call Roz's daughter and let her know what happened."

"She's already been called," said Dr. Robbins. "Roz had that contact information in her purse. Roberta is flying down first thing tomorrow morning."

"Good," said Nora. She gestured toward her brother-in-law. "Vin talked to the police. They think somebody deliberately forced Roz off the road."

Dr. Robbins looked with concern at Vin. "Do they have any idea who?"

"Some fisherman said he saw a dark-colored car," said Vin, "but the guy didn't get a tag or have any other details to offer."

Dr. Robbins sighed and shook his head. "You'd think after all these years I'd get used to seeing people injured, but I don't. It's a little easier, though, when it's a relative stranger. Roz is such a sweet old gal, it's especially hard to see her brutalized."

Chapter 40

In his small room, Levi lay on his bed staring at the ceiling. He had looked everywhere he could think of and still couldn't find his phone. The only place left to search was the place he most feared to go. Tomorrow he would have to force himself to return to the beach and look for it near Shelley's grave.

He closed his eyes and said a silent prayer. For Shelley and for the safety of his sister, Miriam.

He had to head out to Siesta Beach anyway to deliver the hex sign. He hoped Piper would be satisfied. It was unlike any he had ever done.

Some of the symbols he'd chosen were different from ones he'd painted in the past. The heart was obviously appropriate. And the turtles represented the creatures that had brought Kathy and Dan together.

The teardrops could be interpreted as the vicissitudes of life that a married couple had to survive. The birds with their red breasts seemed to symbolize spring and rebirth.

It had been cathartic to paint it. Levi was relieved to have expressed something so important with his art. Something that would last well after he was gone.

He was startled by a loud, insistent banging. He could hear his father grumbling on the other side of the bedroom wall as he shuffled down the hallway to answer the front door.

Levi strained to hear the men's voices. He could make out a few words. Phone. Beach. Son. Then he heard his father's footsteps coming toward his room. The bedroom door opened.

"Levi?" called his father as he held up a battery-operated lantern to light the room. "Wake up, son."

Levi sat up in bed, his heart pounding, his cheeks hot. "What is it, Father?"

"It is the sheriff's deputies, Levi. They say they found a phone that belongs to you."

Levi's mother appeared in the doorway, wrapping her heavy robe tightly around her. Her hair fell long and loose over her shoulders, so different from the bun and bonnet she wore during the day. Her eyes were wide in alarm as she took hold of her husband's arm.

"What is wrong, Abram?"

"Go back to bed, Fannie."

"Tell me," she insisted. "What is wrong?"

"Fannie, please, go back to bed. Levi has to get dressed."

"Now?" she asked with trepidation. "Why?"

"He has to go with the deputies to the sheriff's station."

Chapter 41

Back in her room at the inn, Piper kicked off her sandals, collapsed on the bed, and called Jack.

"First, I *love* the flowers, Jack," she said. "They're beautiful, and my room smells heavenly. Thank you."

"You're welcome. I wish I were down there to see them—and you."

"Me, too," said Piper. "But it won't be long now. It's crazy down here, Jack."

As she reviewed the details of the day, she realized how good it felt to unburden herself. She also realized how good it was to hear his voice.

"I'll make a few calls in the morning and see what I can find out," said Jack after she recounted the grisly scene on the beach and the old woman's accident.

"I think the two things must be related, Jack. I don't think it's a coincidence that Roz was run off the road on the same day as Shelley's body was found. Roz may have seen Shelley's killer carrying her body a few nights ago. The killer might know that and want to get rid of the person who could identify him."

"Did she actually see the man's face?" asked Jack.

"Not really," said Piper. "But *he* doesn't know that."

"Listen, Pipe. If what you think is true, then you've got a dangerous guy lurking around down there. Don't get any big ideas about getting involved. Let the cops do their thing."

"You sound just like my father."

"Smart guy, your dad. Do what he says and stay out of it."

Wednesday

Even though you can hide from the earth,
heaven sees you act.
AMISH PROVERB

Chapter 42

In the interrogation room, Levi sat with his head down. His face was flushed and perspiration dotted his forehead. His hands were clasped together on the table in front of him to keep them from shaking.

"I know I lost my phone," he explained to the detective. "But I did not lose it on the beach. I was not anywhere near the beach. I do not know why you found it there."

Levi knew it was a sin to lie, yet he had to maintain his innocence. It was obvious now, after several hours of interrogation, that the police thought *he* had killed Shelley. This was all an incredible, horrible nightmare.

"Well, how do you explain it?" asked the detective.

"I have told you over and over!" Levi cried as he rested his head on the table. "I just do not know. Maybe somebody found it and left it there."

"Why would someone do that?" asked the detective. "Were they trying to set you up?"

"I do not know," said Levi. He closed his eyes, wishing he could just fall asleep and escape the ceaseless barrage of questions and the sickening feeling he'd carried with him since the night that Shelley was buried.

The detective rose from his chair and left the room. Levi wasn't sure if the man had taken pity on him and wanted to give him a break or if the detective's departure was part of a calculated plan to give Levi time to think and reconsider his answers. Whatever the reason, Levi was grateful to be left alone.

He imagined his parents, waiting at home and worried to death. Theirs was a small community, and news spread fast. Soon everyone would know that the police had taken him in for questioning. Everyone would be speculating on Levi's involvement in a woman's murder and grotesque burial. His parents would be mortified.

But, again, it was the fate of his sister that concerned Levi more. He loved Miriam and would do anything to protect her. Levi wouldn't ever be able to reveal what he knew, because doing so could lead to her death. He had no reason to doubt that the murderer would make good on his threat to find a way to kill Miriam if Levi identified him.

The killer wanted nothing more than to eliminate any witnesses; the police wanted to solve their case. As he waited for the detective to return, Levi decided to go through with what he had only been considering before. He could do something that would satisfy both the killer *and* the police.

The detective entered the room. "You can go for now," he announced. "But don't leave town. We're going to want to talk to you again." He motioned to Levi. "Come on, get up. We'll drive you home."

"No thank you," said Levi, thinking of his parents' humiliation when a police car dropped off their son. "I can get home on my own."

When he walked out of the station, the sun was just coming up. As he headed toward Pinecraft, Levi's resolve strengthened. Though he hated to saddle his parents with the stigma and pain, he wanted to protect Miriam. He also ached to be released from the mental agony he was enduring. The thought of an entire lifetime of this ahead—of looking over his shoulder, of worrying about the killer harming his sister—filled him with dread. It would be better all around to end the whole thing.

He would take responsibility for Shelley's murder.

Chapter 43

The alarm went off way too early. Cryder instantly remembered the late night at the hospital. Before he went in for office hours, he wanted to check on Roz.

With his eyes still closed, Cryder reached out beside him and felt the empty space. Umiko had already gone for her morning walk. She very rarely missed it.

He had to hand it to his wife. She was incredibly disciplined. With her exercise, with her diet, with her housekeeping and careful budgeting. Even when his practice had been young, Umiko had managed to create a seemingly more affluent lifestyle than their income warranted. Now, though they had much more money, she didn't want to move to a bigger or more luxurious place. Umiko was very satisfied with their two-bedroom, one-and-a-half-bath town house. It was their magnificent view of the Gulf of Mexico that she loved and never wanted to leave. Her parents must have sensed that when they named her: Umiko means "child of the sea."

Location, location, location.

Umiko recited the real-estate chant whenever he brought up the subject of selling the place to Walter Engel. Cryder was more than willing to take the profit they would realize and find something else. Maybe an all-on-one-level condo downtown in a high-rise with a marina view. Something newer, with more space, and closer to his office would suit him just fine.

But Umiko was adamantly against selling. She wept whenever he mentioned the subject. Cryder wasn't going to insist that his wife give up the place that made her so happy. He owed her that much. Umiko had already followed him around the world. It hadn't always been easy for her.

But Walter Engel was persistent. He was determined to persuade the Robbinses and everyone else in the complex to sell their places to him. Cryder knew that Roz Golubock was also one of the holdouts.

Getting out of bed, he went to the picture window. He stared out, trying to spot Umiko. He recognized her wide-brimmed hat and slim figure down on the beach where Shelley Hart's body had been found the day before. Cryder was certain that even a murder wasn't going to convince Umiko to sell.

Chapter 44

Propping the pillows behind her, Piper sat up in bed, grabbed her phone, and went straight to her Facebook page. She read through the comments that friends had written in response to the picture of the crime scene she'd posted the day before. Most of the twenty-odd comments advised her to be careful. A few asked who the shirtless beefcake was standing at the right side of the photo. One person even commented on Brad's tattoo:

AS A TATTOO LOVER MYSELF, I ZOOMED IN TO SEE WHAT WAS ON THE HUNK'S ARM. MY BET IS THAT GUY HAS DONE TIME. HE GOT THAT TAT IN PRISON.

Good catch, thought Piper. She was reminded again of how increasingly difficult it was to get away with anything, what with better and better technology and a global village watching.

She clicked on the television in time to hear the weatherman describing what people on Florida's western coast could expect. Another day of sunshine with temperatures in the seventies.

It had amused her years ago to notice how local news broadcasts here led with the weather forecast. She eventually realized that this was because the weather was so important to almost every Sarasota viewer. The threat of rain or an upcoming cold snap was of immense interest both to farmers and to businesses that depended on tourism. And of course tourists were interested, too.

But it was the story after the weather that Piper wanted to hear. The only new detail being revealed to the public was the identity of the woman's body found on Siesta Beach. Shelley Hart was described as a lifelong Sarasota resident. Police were asking anyone with information on the case to come forward.

The following item wasn't an actual edited news package. It was merely video voiced over by the anchorperson. The pictures showed a mangled yellow convertible being lifted onto a flatbed truck.

"Also on Siesta Key, a car driven by an Ocean Boulevard homeowner crashed at the base of the North Bridge last night. The driver, eighty-seven-year-old

Roz Golubock, was taken to Memorial Hospital. Police say the convertible may have been deliberately run off the road by another car. They are looking for witnesses."

Piper turned off the set. Shelley's sandy grave, Roz's treacherous crash. Would the police be able to solve the cases only if witnesses came forward with something they had seen?

As she got out of bed, Piper instinctively felt that there was just one person who knew all the details of each case. The person responsible for both.

Chapter 45

With her three children scampering around the small kitchen, Jo-Jo Williams opened the refrigerator and pulled out a gallon container of milk. Almost empty. She made a mental note to get to Walmart as soon as the kids left for school.

Add the milk to a very long list of things they needed. The cupboards were looking pretty darn bare. Try as Jo-Jo did to stretch her dollars, there just never seemed to be enough money to stock the shelves full again.

She hated living paycheck to paycheck and depending on the tips she made at the bar at night. Her credit cards were maxed out, and the bill collectors called on a regular basis now. Even if her baby daddy helped out like he was supposed to but didn't, Jo-Jo doubted she would ever be able to climb completely out of debt.

As she transferred the store-brand puffed rice into bowls, Jo-Jo heard the weather report coming from the little television on the counter. She was glad it was going to be sunny. It was a pain to lug grocery bags in the rain.

She poured the milk over the cereal, carefully dividing it three ways. The kids sat down and began to hungrily devour their breakfast. Jo-Jo noticed that all three of them needed new sneakers.

"The dead woman was identified as twenty-seven-year-old Shelley Hart, a lifelong Sarasota resident."

Jo-Jo looked over in time to catch the woman's face on the screen. She gasped as she realized that she recognized her. It was the woman who had come into the bar the other night and sat with that guy in the back. The big tipper.

Chapter 46

"We'll have three round tiers: a fourteen-inch, a ten-inch, and a six-inch. That should serve seventy-five to a hundred ten people."

Piper pushed the shopping cart as her mother reeled off the components necessary to make the wedding cake. Weeks ago Piper and Terri had calculated how much of each ingredient would be needed. Now all they had to do was follow their list.

Pounds of flour, granulated and confectioners' sugar, and unsalted butter were placed in the basket, followed by a large bottle of pure vanilla extract, a couple of cartons of eggs, and several containers of whole milk. After picking up a box of baking soda, they headed for the produce section, where they selected a mesh bag full of key limes.

"That should do it," said Terri as she surveyed the contents of the shopping cart.

"Wait, we forgot the toothpicks," said Piper. "You go get in line, Mom, and I'll run and grab some."

As she turned the corner, Piper bumped into a man coming around from the next aisle.

"Oh, excuse me," she said as she looked up. She was startled to see Brad O'Hara's face. His expression instantly changed from annoyance to pleasure.

"And to think I was expecting this to be a lousy morning," said Brad.

Again, to Piper, his mouth seemed to be leering more than grinning. And the tattoo of the crying woman on his arm was really freaking her out.

"Oh, yeah, hi. Sorry, my mother is waiting for me at the checkout," said Piper as she managed a weak smile. "I've got to hurry."

"You've got to relax, Piper," he said as he reached over and grabbed her arm. "Slow down and enjoy life. Let me take you for a kayak ride today."

Piper pulled away, shrugged, and managed to say, "I can't. Remember? We've got that cruise on the bay this afternoon."

As she walked off, Piper could well understand why Shelley hadn't wanted to have anything to do with him.

Chapter 47

It took him just over an hour to walk home. His mouth was dry, and his eyes burned. Levi spent the time figuring out how he was going to get everything accomplished. There was so much to do.

First he had to face his parents. He dreaded seeing the bewilderment and worry in their eyes. He had never wanted to cause them any pain. He hated to think they were in for still more.

Then he had to finish the hex sign. With no interruptions he could complete it this morning and deliver it to Piper Donovan after the restaurant's lunch crowd left. Since this was going to be the last lunch he worked at Fisher's, Levi wanted to stay and help as long as he was needed.

As he walked along Bahia Vista, Levi was oblivious to the cars speeding by and the sun's increasing intensity. Instead he noticed the weeds sticking out from cracks in the sidewalk and the scuff marks on the toes of his black shoes. Head down, step by step, Levi mentally composed the letter he was going to write.

That was going to be the most challenging task of all. It had to be carefully worded. How to explain things in such a way that it kept Miriam safe yet ended the nightmare for good?

Chapter 48

Piper dropped her mother off at the front door of the inn and then drove around to the service entrance. As she started unloading the grocery bags from the trunk of the car, she heard a male voice. She looked around but didn't see anyone. The voice seemed to be coming from the side of the building.

Paying little attention, she lifted two bags from the trunk and began walking toward the door to the kitchen. She stiffened when she thought she heard the voice say, "Shelley."

Piper stopped and strained to listen. She couldn't hear clearly. Many of the words were muted by distance and the wall. Quietly she put down her bags and edged closer to the corner of the building.

"She was complicating everything."

A pause followed. Piper assumed that the man was having a phone conversation.

"I'm just glad she's out of the way," he said. "I don't appreciate being threatened."

Who was that? Piper wanted to peek around the corner, but she held herself in check. What if whoever was talking saw her? He certainly wouldn't be pleased that she'd overheard his conversation.

She decided to go back to the car and continue as if she was unloading it. If she waited a bit, he would finish his phone call and should pass right by her.

Piper glanced up to see Isaac Goode coming around the corner. He looked happily surprised to see her. If he had anything to hide, it wasn't apparent in the bright smile he directed her way.

"Let me help you with those," said Isaac when he saw the packages.

"Thanks," said Piper.

Between the two of them, they carried everything into the kitchen in three trips. Isaac assisted in emptying the bags, putting away the things that needed to be refrigerated and organizing the dry ingredients on an empty counter.

"You know, this is the first time I've encountered this situation," said Isaac.

Piper looked at him quizzically. "What situation?"

"Guests making the wedding cake. I like to patronize the bakery I always use. I know they're dependable and do a wonderful job. When Kathy told me she wanted you and your mother to make her cake, I wasn't exactly thrilled."

"You don't have to worry," said Piper. "My mother has been doing this for years."

Isaac nodded. "That's what Kathy said. And then she showed me the picture of the cake you made for that star of *A Little Rain Must Fall,* and I felt better. I adore that show. I've been watching it since I was a kid. I used to have a friend of mine tape it for me, and then I'd sneak over to her house to watch. I grew up in an Amish family. Nobody was into television."

Piper imagined a young Isaac hiding his interests and proclivities. Growing up must have been rough for him; she felt a pang of empathy. He didn't seem like somebody who would kill anybody.

"What was it like anyway?" he asked. "You know . . . being with all those soap people?"

"It was fun," she said. "I wish I could have spent more time with them."

"I remember when you were on there for a while," said Isaac. "Mariah Lane. I hated when they killed you off."

"That makes two of us," said Piper.

She watched as he turned to stow a carton of eggs in the refrigerator. Piper noticed Isaac's hand trembling as he reached in—the carton slipped and tumbled onto the floor, its contents spilling out.

"What's the matter with me?" he asked as he surveyed the cracked eggs. "What a klutz I am."

"No problem," said Piper, glancing around for a roll of paper towels. "We can always get more eggs."

As they wiped up the gooey mess together, Piper thought Isaac seemed harmless enough. Still, she'd heard him saying he was glad that Shelley wasn't around. What could Shelley have been threatening him with?

Chapter 49

The elevator doors opened at Sarasota Memorial Hospital. A woman with a cloud of dark brown hair and very pale skin, wearing a black sweater and slacks and carrying a large designer handbag, exited the elevator and scanned the wall in front of her for a clue as to which way to go. An arrow indicated that her mother's room was to the right.

Roberta Golubock winced as she saw the frail woman lying with her eyes closed in the hospital bed. A bandage covered her forehead, there were abrasions on her cheeks, and her lip was swollen to three times its normal size. Her mother's thin arms rested on top of the cotton blanket. They were mottled with angry bruises.

Quietly Roberta lifted a chair and placed it next to the bed. Glancing at her watch, she sat down, took out her iPad, and began reading. Half an hour later, her mother still hadn't opened her eyes.

Walking out to the nurses' station, Roberta waited until one of them looked her way.

"Hi, I'm Roz Golubock's daughter. Has the doctor been in yet to see my mother this morning?"

"Room 321, right?" asked the nurse as she steered the mouse and focused on the computer screen. "Yes, Dr. Robbins was in and saw her earlier."

"And?" asked Roberta.

"He ordered a CT scan, which she's already had. It was normal."

Roberta exhaled with relief. "Oh, that's good news. So now what?"

The nurse looked at the screen again. "Well, he hasn't ordered her release yet."

"How can I talk with him?" asked Roberta.

"I'll page him," said the nurse.

Turning away from the station, Roberta peeked into her mother's room again and saw that she was now sitting up in bed.

"Hey there, sleepyhead." Roberta gave Roz a kiss on the forehead. "How are you, Mother?"

Roz squinted. There was a puzzled look on her face.

Roberta sat on the edge of the bed and gently took Roz's hand. "Mother? It's me. Roberta."

The older woman pulled away. "I don't know you," she said firmly. "Who are you?"

In the hall outside her mother's hospital room, Roberta listened intently as the doctor explained the situation.

"It seems as if Roz is suffering from a retrograde amnesia," said Dr. Robbins. "It's the loss of preexisting memories, starting with the most recent ones. The fact that your mother didn't recognize you or me would seem to suggest that she has a more severe case."

"Is this because she hit her head during the accident?" asked Roberta. "I thought the CT scan was normal."

"It was," said Cryder, "but amnesia can occur without any anatomical damage to the brain. We call that a psychogenic amnesia. A traumatic situation that the individual wants to consciously or unconsciously avoid can trigger it."

Roberta's brow wrinkled. "So the accident was so traumatic for my mother that her brain is blocking it out?"

"Perhaps," said Cryder. "Either the accident or something else. It's hard to say."

"How long does this sort of amnesia last?" asked Roberta. "And what can be done about it? Should I try to remind her of people and events?"

"You can if you want," said the doctor, "but that hasn't been shown to have any scientific bearing on recovering memory. Fortunately, memory usually returns on its own."

Roberta digested the information. "Okay, so this is just going to take some time, right?"

"Yes, other than the amnesia, Roz is doing remarkably well, especially for someone her age. She's in very good health."

Roberta nodded. "She's always taken care of herself. I guess that's paying off now. When can she go home?"

"Let's keep her here another night, just to be on the safe side. But when she goes home, she should really have someone with her."

"I'll be able to stay through the weekend," said Roberta. "After that I'll get someone to come in if she needs it. Nevertheless, who knows? Maybe the amnesia will be gone by then."

"Let's hope so," said Cryder.

Roberta extended her hand. "Thank you, Dr. Robbins. I appreciate your taking such good care of my mother. She's told me how you help so many people in the town houses. I've always been glad that there's a doctor so close by. Especially now. I was reading on my iPad about that horrible thing on the beach. Between that and the fact that it looks as though my mother was run off the road, I'm very worried about what's going on down here."

Chapter 50

Piper knocked on the door of her parents' room. Her father answered, with his finger to his lips. She looked inside and saw that her mother was on the telephone. By the expression on her mother's face, Piper could tell that something was wrong.

"Is this a temporary thing, Nora?" asked Terri. "Or does the doctor think the amnesia will last?"

Piper assumed that her mother was talking to her aunt about Roz Golubock. She watched as Terri nodded and listened to the answer.

"I'll go over to the hospital with you," Terri offered. She paced across the room while listening to the response.

"All right, if that's what you want, Nora. I'll talk to you when we get back."

Terri hung up and looked at her husband and daughter. "Roz has something called posttraumatic amnesia. She doesn't remember what happened right before the accident, and she seems to have lost knowledge of who people are. Her daughter flew down from New York this morning, and Roz didn't even recognize her."

"Well?" asked Vin. "What did Nora say? *Is* it temporary?"

Terri shrugged. "Everybody hopes so, but who knows? Nora is driving over to the hospital in a little while to talk more with Roz's daughter. But she wants us to go ahead with the bay cruise this afternoon as planned."

"Man, the guy who ran Roz off the road should be turning cartwheels," observed Piper. "The woman he almost killed can't give the police any info to help find him."

Chapter 51

On her way to Walmart, Jo-Jo made a detour. Though she wasn't scheduled in until five o'clock, she wanted to stop at the bar. No one would be there this early, giving her the opportunity to find what she needed.

A few blocks from the Alligator Alley Bar & Grill, Jo-Jo parked in front of a sidewalk newspaper-vending machine. Through the glass pull-down window, she could see the headline:

WOMAN FOUND BURIED ON SIESTA KEY BEACH

Jo-Jo inserted her quarters into the coin slot, took out a newspaper, and got back into the car. She scanned the front-page article, which stated that Shelley Hart had last been seen at the Whispering Sands Inn. Jo-Jo reached for one of her kids' broken crayons on the car floor and underlined the sentence. Her ability to disprove that bit of misinformation was going to earn her fifty thousand dollars. Carefully tearing the article from the newspaper, she scrawled *"AA B&G"* in the margin. Then she tucked the article into the visor.

When she arrived at the bar, she noticed a pile of cigarette butts littering the area outside the rear door. Jo-Jo's key slid easily into the lock. As she walked into the darkened room, she was hit by the stale smell of beer. She headed straight for the alarm panel, pressing the code to disarm it.

Jo-Jo entered the owner's tiny office. The room was a mess. Catalogs were haphazardly stacked on the floor. Bills and receipts were strewn all over the desk. The trash basket was overflowing with empty cans and take-out containers.

The owner insisted on doing everything himself. He clearly could use some housekeeping and clerical assistance. Hoping to earn a little extra cash, Jo-Jo had volunteered to help. For a while she had. But when the owner realized she wanted to get paid extra, he told her to stop.

Still, Jo-Jo had gained some knowledge of how his so-called filing system worked. She went to the dented metal cabinet and pulled out the bottom drawer. She found the folder stuffed with credit-card receipts.

Since most of the bar's business was conducted with cash, it didn't take much time to riffle through the paper-thin rectangles. Jo-Jo found the one she was looking for. She recognized it by the date and because she noted the 100 percent tip.

Wow!

Jo-Jo remembered wishing she had a guy in her life who was such a sport. She'd envied the pretty woman in the yellow sweater who sat across from him.

Jo-Jo certainly didn't envy her anymore.

Chapter 52

The awning-covered pontoon boat docked at Mote Marine Aquarium stood ready to take on the wedding guests. The bridegroom himself planned to conduct the two-hour cruise through Sarasota and Roberts bays. The Donovans settled themselves into seats near the rear.

Piper recognized some of the people boarding the boat along with quite a few she hadn't seen before. She watched as Isaac Goode, dressed in white slacks, a navy sport shirt, and a nautical cap, carried a large cooler and deposited it on the deck. Piper was surprised to see Walter Engel, since Aunt Nora wasn't joining the cruise. To Piper's dismay, Brad O'Hara took the seat in front of her.

Piper observed Umiko and Cryder Robbins boarding the boat. Immediately the physician was barraged with questions about Roz Golubock.

"She's resting comfortably," he said. "She'll likely be released tomorrow. Her daughter is with her now."

Terri leaned over and whispered to her husband and daughter, "It's a good sign the doctor is making this boat ride. He can't be too concerned about Roz."

Vin shook his head. "It takes a lot for these guys to miss their Wednesday afternoons off."

As the pontoon pulled away from the pier, Kathy and Dan stood at the front. They each stepped up to the microphone to welcome their guests. Though Kathy smiled, Piper could see the strain in her cousin's face. Piper marveled that she was holding it together at all, given the horrific events of the last few days.

"For the next two hours, we want you to chill out as we travel through the waters of our beloved Sarasota," said Dan. "I'll be giving you a running commentary on the history, ecology, and folklore of the area. We'll make a stop for a short nature walk on an uninhabited island, and we'll float by a rookery so you can see pelicans, herons, ibis, and egrets in their nesting habitats."

Kathy took the microphone from her fiancé. "Keep an eye out for the bottlenose dolphins, everybody. Sometimes they come right up to the boat."

Piper relaxed and gazed out at the turquoise water as the boat sped up. A cool breeze blew across her face, whipping her hair behind her. She was grateful for the blue awning overhead that shielded the passengers from the sun's damaging rays.

Dan held the microphone to his mouth. "Hunting and fishing supported the native populations here for thousands of years as Florida attracted some of the earliest human settlements in this hemisphere. In the 1500s the Europeans arrived in the area, and by the turn of the twentieth century, Sarasota was still mainly a fishing village with a very small population, unpaved streets, and fish houses on the bay front. The last hundred years have witnessed Sarasota's transformation into the cosmopolitan and cultural city you see today."

The cruise participants looked out at the glass-and-steel skyscrapers that rimmed the shoreline. Modern and sleek, they stood majestic against the bright blue sky. The boat continued farther out into the bay. Office buildings of the downtown area gave way to residential waterfront properties with big stucco-covered houses, infinity-edge swimming pools, and yachts moored at private piers.

"Oh, look!" shouted Piper, pointing out at the water. "There's a dolphin! There's a bunch of them!"

All heads turned in the direction that Piper indicated. One by one, four dorsal fins pierced the water's surface. The dolphins gracefully rose, took in fresh air through their blowholes, and then dove back down again.

"Are they going down there to find something for lunch?" asked Isaac. "What exactly do they eat?"

"Predominantly fish," answered Dan, "but they also enjoy squid and crustaceans. Diet, of course, varies by region, but pinfish account for about seventy percent of what our bottlenose dolphins here in Sarasota eat. An adult male eats about twenty pounds of fish a day, while a nursing mother can eat forty! And they are impressive hunters. I've seen dolphins smack fish clear out of the water with their tails and into the mouths of their podmates."

"Will we see any manatees?" Piper called out.

"Probably not this time of year," said Dan, "but we have lots of them in the summer."

Isaac passed out soft drinks as the cruise continued. Dan talked about the sea life and environmental issues facing the area as the guests enjoyed the ride. About an hour into the trip, the pontoon approached a small parcel of land.

"This is Governors Island," said Dan. "It's uninhabited, but boaters come out here to picnic. I'll be able to show you some interesting plants and points of archaeological interest. We'll stay here for about a half hour. You'll have time to wander around a bit on your own."

The guests disembarked, walking down a small gangplank that led from the deck to the sandy beach.

Piper followed her parents. When she got to the ramp, she saw Brad O'Hara waiting at the bottom. He reached out and took her arm to steady her as she descended.

His grip was tight. Alarmingly tight.

Dan pointed out the tall, wispy trees. "Those are Australian pines, and they are aliens; they don't belong here. Somehow they found their way here from the other side of the world, and they've proliferated to the point they're a serious threat to the Everglades, the Keys, and Florida in general. They're fast-growing and produce thick blankets of leaves and pointed fruits that cover the ground, displacing beach vegetation and destroying habitats for native insects and other wildlife." Dan bent and picked up a branchlet of scalelike leaves that resembled pine needles and passed it around.

"These buggers radically alter the light, temperature, and soil chemistry of our beaches. Their thick, shallow roots make the trees much more susceptible to blow over during high winds, leading to increased beach and dune erosion and interference with the nesting activities of our sea turtles."

"Why doesn't the government just cut them down and burn them?" asked Walter.

"I'm afraid it's too late for that," answered Dan. "They're everywhere now. We can't stop the invasion."

As they all took the remaining time to explore the small island on their own, Piper sought out Dan.

"Having fun?" he asked.

"Yeah," she said, "it's a blast. And you really know what you're talking about, Dan."

"Thanks, Piper. I just think this stuff rocks." He bent forward. "What's that on your arm?" he asked.

Piper glanced down, noticing the red marks on the white skin of her upper arm. She gently rubbed the spot.

"Your friend Brad helped me off the boat," she answered.

Dan shook his head. "Brad doesn't know his own strength sometimes."

"Okay, Dan. This might be totally none of my business, but why are you friends with somebody like that? A drug dealer?"

"You know about that?"

"Mm-hmm. He admitted it to the police at the beach when he identified Shelley's body."

"Yeah, I'm sure Brad will be in the cops' crosshairs because of his history with Shelley. Her testimony sent him to prison. Her little brother overdosed on the stuff Brad sold to him."

"What a nightmare," groaned Piper.

"It was," said Dan. "But we go way back. I've known him since we were kids, and there's been a lot of stuff over the years. He's not all bad. And he's paid his debt to society. You don't get rid of a lifelong friend because he's less than perfect, right? Everybody has faults."

"Who has faults?" asked Kathy as she joined them.

"Certainly not you," said Dan, putting his arm around her and kissing his fiancée on the forehead. He lowered his voice. "We were talking about Brad."

"I feel kinda sorry for him," said Kathy. "He's got that criminal record, but he's trying to live an honest life now. At least we *think* he is."

Dan walked ahead to start rounding up the passengers. Piper and Kathy lingered.

"This feels so weird," Kathy confided. "Part of me is so happy to be marrying Dan in just three days and to have everybody here to celebrate it. But then there's the other part of me that can't believe Shelley is dead. And no one knows what actually happened to Roz. This is not how I imagined things."

Piper hugged her cousin. "I know," she said reassuringly. "But the police are working on it. And I told my friend Jack, who's in the FBI, and he's trying to find out what's happening, too. The truth will come out, Kathy. You'll see."

The pontoon traveled out into the bay again.

"Those pelicans look like they're on kamikaze missions," observed Vin as he watched a prehistoric-looking bird dive straight into the water. When the pelican came to the surface, its throat pouch was wiggling as the captured fish struggled inside.

"And now to what I consider the highlight of the cruise," said Dan into the microphone. "We're going to do some trawling!"

He lowered a bucket attached to a rope into the bay. While the boat pulled the bucket behind it for a while, the guests gathered around a portable aquarium. Dan finally pulled the bucket up and dumped the contents into the glass-walled box.

Everyone exclaimed in delight and wonder at the randomly captured sea life. A tiny sea horse, two sea urchins, a small snook, a ladyfish, three large shrimps, and some sponge and sea grass. Dan put on gloves and took each item out, talked about it, and offered it to anyone who wanted to touch it.

"What is *that*?" asked Piper, pointing to the bloated round creature covered with pointed spines.

"It's a puffer fish," Vin declared.

"Yes," said Dan, pleased that Vin remembered his lecture at Mote the day before. Dan reached into the tank and pulled it out. "It has an extremely elastic stomach, and if it senses a threat, it inflates itself with water or air as a defense mechanism. It's very smart, really. An unsuspecting predator finds itself facing an unappetizing pointy ball rather than a tasty meal. Although if it knew what some puffer fish contain, the predator would stay away."

"What do you mean?" asked Piper as she took out her phone to snap a picture.

Dan held out the globe-shaped fish and turned it from side to side so everybody could get a good view of it. "Some of these little beauties are generally believed to be among the most poisonous vertebrates in the world," he said. "Even though certain internal organs, like the liver and sometimes the skin, are highly toxic when eaten, in Asia the meat is considered a delicacy. It must be prepared by chefs who know which part is safe to eat and in what quantity. Otherwise it's lethal."

"What makes it so deadly?" asked Piper.

"We think the toxicity comes from their diet, because puffer fish born and grown in captivity don't make the poison. When they ingest certain bacteria from the shellfish prey they eat in the wild, the toxins develop. We're doing experiments on this now."

Chapter 53

*E*avesdroppers learned very valuable information, even on a deserted island.

Piper Donovan had a big mouth and an even bigger ego. Where did she get off swooping in from the north and interfering down here? Piper was quite the little busybody, wasn't she?

The FBI? Kathy's cousin had the FBI looking into Shelley's murder and the old lady's accident? It was bad enough having the Sarasota sheriff's department all over both things. He certainly didn't need any additional attention from the Federal Bureau of Investigation. He suspected that even a couple of phone calls from the feds would increase the law-enforcement heat.

The news media weren't helping either. Plastering Shelley's face all over the place couldn't be good. It could *jog somebody's memory—somebody who might have noticed her with him at the bar that night. Though it was dark and crowded and the patrons were feeling no pain, somebody might remember the striking-looking woman who sat with him in the booth at the back.*

As for Roz, he hoped the media reports wouldn't jog anybody's memory in that regard either. Luckily, he'd been able to get the yellow paint off his car using the bottle of compounding solution and the can of wax in his trunk. It hadn't been necessary to bring the car into a body shop, where some mechanic might ask questions and put two and two together.

Though he hadn't accomplished his goal with Roz, her amnesia was a huge gift. For the time being, she didn't remember anything. Later he could finish the job.

And there was the other matter to worry about, the one that Shelley had threatened him with in the first place. Shelley had put her pretty little nose where it didn't belong. Now Piper Donovan was doing the very same thing.

Chapter 54

Vin and Terri got off the boat first with Walter. They were returning to Whispering Sands Inn together.

Piper hung back to ride with Kathy and Dan. While the bride and groom discussed something with the wedding planner, Piper chatted with Dr. and Mrs. Robbins. She tried to ignore the fact that Brad O'Hara was planted on his seat on the pontoon. Piper could feel him watching her.

Finally Kathy looked over and smiled. "Piper, would you mind if we stopped at the tiki hut? Isaac wants to show us how the tables will be arranged for the rehearsal dinner Friday night."

"Sure. I'd like to see it." Piper got up, unmindful of the water that had pooled on the deck when the bucket of Gulf creatures had been hoisted aboard. She took a few steps and slipped. She tumbled forward, her leg smashing down on the tip of a metal docking cleat.

Piper cried out as the stabbing pain shot through her body. She looked at her leg and saw bright red blood spreading over her skin. Her eyes filled with tears.

"Oh, no!" cried Kathy, rushing to her cousin and kneeling next to her. Immediately Piper was surrounded by a circle of the passengers still on the boat.

"Let me see," said Dr. Robbins. He bent over to examine Piper's leg, his eyes narrowing as he scrutinized the damage. "When was your last tetanus shot?"

Piper shook her head. "I really can't remember."

Dr. Robbins looked up at Dan. "There must be a first-aid kit on board, right?"

"Of course," answered Dan. "I'll get it."

The doctor wiped away the blood and applied disinfectant to the cut. "You're lucky, Piper. You may not need stitches. We can probably close this up with some Dermabond. But for sure let's go to my office for a tetanus shot."

"I'll go with you," said Brad. "I want to help."

Before Piper or anyone else could respond, Brad swept her up in his arms and carried her off the boat.

As Piper was buckling her belt in the front seat of Brad's car, Kathy ran up to her window.

"I'll go with you, Piper. Dan and I will drive you over and take you home later."

Piper didn't want to go with Brad. She also appreciated that Kathy was volunteering to drop everything in order take care of her. But Piper didn't want to make a big deal out of a relatively small accident. Her cousin had already had way too much stress leading up to her wedding day.

"It's all right, Kathy." She managed a smile. "You and Dan go ahead and check out the preps at the tiki hut. I'm fine. Really."

"You sure?" asked Kathy. She made an almost imperceptible nod toward Brad, signaling that she knew Piper was uncomfortable with him.

"Really, Kath. I'm sure. I'll see you later."

When they reached the medical building, Brad parked the car and ran around to open Piper's door. He leaned in, his arms outstretched.

"No thanks," said Piper. "I can walk."

Within seconds Dr. Robbins and his wife pulled into the lot and parked beside them. As they strode across the macadam, Piper noticed a well-dressed man waiting in front of the office.

"Oh, no," said Umiko. "Doesn't he realize you don't have office hours this afternoon?"

"I'm sure he doesn't really care, sweetheart," said Cryder. "When people think they need a doctor, they don't care if it's his time off. In fact, they resent it."

"What should we tell him?" asked Umiko.

"We're here now. No sense turning him away. I'll see him after Piper."

As Dr. Robbins inserted his key into the office door, Piper noticed Brad and the waiting man exchanging looks. Though neither man spoke, she sensed they definitely recognized each other.

All done," said Cryder as he capped the tube of medical glue and surveyed his work. "You'll hardly be able to see it when it heals."

"Great," said Piper, looking down at her leg. "I appreciate it, Dr. Robbins."

"Cryder, Piper. You can call me Cryder. It's going to hurt for a while, and you'll probably be pretty sore tonight from the fall. Come into my office. I want to write you a prescription for pain."

"Do you really think I'll need it?" asked Piper as she followed him. "Can't I just take Tylenol or something?"

Cryder frowned as he picked up the prescription pad from his desk. "Damn. This is the last sheet. Again."

"See?" said Piper. "You're meant to save it for that other patient."

"All right," Cryder said uncertainly. "If you think you can get by with some acetaminophen, fine. But if it really starts to bother you, I'm just down the road. Your aunt has my home number."

Piper glanced down at the desk, noticing the line of precisely arranged carved figurines. "Oh, these are great!" she exclaimed.

Cryder smiled with pleasure. "They're called netsuke. They were used as toggles and fasteners on kimonos. They evolved over time from being strictly utilitarian into objects of great artistry and craftsmanship."

"May I?" asked Piper.

"Sure, go ahead."

She picked up an inch-tall fisherman, complete with pole and tiny fish. "I can even see the look of satisfaction on his face. Amazing!"

"I started collecting them when I was stationed in Japan when I was in the navy. They've become a passion of mine. I've got quite a collection now, here and at home."

Piper returned the netsuke to its place on the desk. "Is that where you and your wife met?" she asked.

"Yes," said Cryder. "She was working on the base. I fell in love with her the instant I saw her."

"That's so romantic," said Piper. "I love hearing a story like that."

"He didn't give you anything for pain?" asked Brad incredulously as he drove Piper back to Siesta Key. "I hate it when docs are stingy with the pain meds."

"He wanted to," said Piper, "but I said I didn't think I'd need it."

"I bet that's a first for him," said Brad.

"What do you mean?"

"Who doesn't take a prescription for pain when they can get one? Not anybody I know."

"Well, now you know somebody," said Piper.

He steered the car off the highway.

"What are you doing?" asked Piper.

"I'm going into the CVS and get you extra-strength Tylenol and some ice packs. At least you should have those in case it hurts during the night."

"All right," said Piper, reaching for her purse. "I guess that's a good idea."

She withdrew her wallet, but Brad was already out of the car. Piper watched as he strode into the pharmacy. It was sweet, really, that he was concerned about her

well-being. Brad had been very protective as he'd carried her to the car after she fell and cut herself. Now he
was being thoughtful and solicitous.

Maybe Dan was right. A prison stretch gave a person
time to think and take stock. Perhaps Brad was really
trying to lead an honest life now. Piper wondered if she
should give him another chance.

Chapter 55

Piper's parents were sitting in the lobby when Brad dropped her off at the inn. Levi Fisher was also waiting. There was a very big box at his feet. Piper smiled with pleasure when she saw it.

"Piper, are you all right?" asked Terri as she got up and went to her daughter. "Kathy called and told us what happened."

"I'm fine, Mom. It's no big deal."

Vin eyed the bandage. "You got a tetanus shot, didn't you?"

"Yes, Dad." She tried to keep the impatience from her voice. But when she saw the strain and worry in both her parents' faces, Paper softened. "You've taught me well, Dad. I know that you can't be too careful."

She turned to Levi.

"You finished the hex sign?" she asked.

"Yes," answered Levi. "It is done."

"Can we see it?"

"Of course." Levi leaned over and opened the cardboard box. He carefully lifted the large wooden disk and held it out toward Piper.

"Oh, Levi. It's perfect!" Piper exclaimed. "You are so talented." She turned to her parents. "Isn't this amazing?"

The Donovans enthusiastically began deciphering the meanings of the colorful symbols on the hex sign.

"Look at the little green turtles in the middle," Terri said with delight. "They must stand for the sea turtle season that brought Kathy and Dan together."

"And it's obvious why you painted the heart on there," said Vin. He looked at Levi. "But why those teardrops?"

Before Levi could answer, Piper chimed in. "It goes with the birds, Dad. The tears signify sadness, and the chirping birds signify happiness. Perfect for a married couple who will experience both during their lives together. Isn't that right, Levi?"

"That's at least one way of looking at it," Levi said.

"What about the scallop shell?" asked Piper.

"To the Amish it represents ocean waves, smooth sailing in life," answered Levi.

Piper studied the young man's face. It was pale and expressionless, yet there were beads of perspiration on his forehead. It reminded Piper of the descriptions regarding somebody in shock.

"Is everything all right, Levi?" she asked.

"Yes. But I have to get going. My parents need me at the restaurant."

"All right," Piper said uncertainly as she opened her purse. "How much do I owe you for your beautiful work?"

"I do not want anything," said Levi. "It is for Kathy and Dan, and they have been very good to me and my family."

"Absolutely not," Piper protested. "That's really sweet of you, Levi, but I asked you to make it as *my* gift. I insist on paying you."

Before she could get her wallet out of her bag, Levi hurried away.

Chapter 56

Good thing he couldn't see how she was shaking. Jo-Jo struggled to keep her voice from cracking as she spoke into the phone.

"I served you that night at the bar when you were with Shelley Hart," she said. "I have the credit-card receipt with your name on it. You should have paid in cash."

The man was silent for what seemed to Jo-Jo a long time. She couldn't believe she was actually doing this. Never in her life would she have thought that she would resort to blackmail. But three kids, an empty bank account, and relentless calls from bill collectors changed things.

Finally the man spoke. "What do you want?" he asked.

"Guess," said Jo-Jo.

"How much?"

She almost choked as she spit out the words. "Fifty thousand dollars. I think my silence is well worth that, don't you?"

"You think I can just put my hands on that kind of money?" he asked.

"I don't know, but I'm hoping so," said Jo-Jo. "I take you for a generous sort of person. That was a very nice tip you gave me the other night."

"No good deed goes unpunished," said the man.

"Sorry about that," said Jo-Jo. "I really am. But I got to do what I got to do."

"All right. I could get it to you tonight. Can you come to Siesta Key?"

"I have to work, but I'll see if one of the other girls can cover the end of my shift. Is eleven o'clock too late?"

"Not at all," said the man. "Want to meet at the Beach 7 entrance?"

"No way," said Jo-Jo. "It'll be way too deserted at that time of night. Since the last woman who met you ended up dead, a crowded place would be better. Let's meet at the parking lot in front of the Siesta Market. I'll be driving a beat-up green Impala with an American flag on the antenna. You won't be able to miss it."

Chapter 57

Piper hobbled after Levi, catching up with him in the parking area as he got on his bicycle.

"Hey!" she called. "Levi, listen. If I don't pay you for the hex sign, it's a wedding present from you, not from me."

Levi took his feet off the pedals and put them down on the macadam. He looked at the ground and shook his head slowly. His wide-brimmed hat shaded his face, but Piper could still see the anguish on it.

"It does not feel right for me to take money for it," he said softly.

"Why?" asked Piper. "I totally get that you care about Kathy and Dan, but that doesn't mean you shouldn't get paid for something *I* asked you to make for them."

"It is not just for them," murmured Levi.

"What do you mean?" asked Piper. "Who else would it be for?"

Levi raised his head and looked directly at Piper. "Never mind. I just cannot take your money for it."

Before Piper could press the wad of cash into his hand, Levi pedaled away.

Chapter 58

Since the police had kept his cell phone, Levi had to find another way to contact the man who'd threatened his sister's life. It wasn't easy to find a pay phone anymore, but Levi seemed to remember that there was one outside the 7-Eleven in Siesta Village. He rode his bike there and parked it out in front.

A girl wearing shorts and a bikini top walked out of the convenience store, sipping on a Slurpee. She winked at him as she passed. Levi felt his face grow hot.

His heart pounded as he inserted the coins and punched the numbers on the keypad. But as the seconds ticked by before he heard the voice of Shelley's killer, Levi began to feel weirdly detached. He was watching the whole thing, not really a part of it anymore. Since he had come up with his plan, the ache in his head and the tightness in his chest had abated. Now he felt strange, as if he were on autopilot.

"I just wanted you to know that the police think I did it," Levi said in a flat tone. "And it is best for everyone if they continue to think that. I am going to take responsibility for it. You are safe, and there is nothing to worry about. I just want you to promise me that you will not hurt Miriam."

"You'd do that?" asked the voice. "I can't believe you'd actually take responsibility for a crime you didn't commit, something that would send you to prison for a very long time—or worse."

"I do not care about prison. I care about my sister."

"Florida has the death penalty, you know."

"I know that," said Levi.

Chapter 59

*I*t was the last thing in the world he had expected. A fabulous piece of luck. But was it too good to be true?

Would Levi actually do it? Would he really take the rap for Shelley's murder? Or would he crack under the pressures he was surely going to face? Between the police, prison, and possibly death row, would the kid recant and reveal the truth?

From what he knew of Levi and the way he'd been raised, the odds were the kid would try to keep his word. The fact that Levi was petrified of having something happen to his sister made it even more unlikely that he would tell the authorities what he knew. Chances were decent that Levi wasn't going to betray him.

At the very least, for now, the responsibility Levi was taking bought time. But he was getting ahead of himself. First he had to deal with the waitress. Unlike Levi, blackmailers couldn't be trusted.

Chapter 60

When Piper went back inside the inn, her parents were still in the lobby.

"Did you pay him?" asked Vin.

"He wouldn't let me," said Piper. "I tried, but he wouldn't take it. I'm going to wait a little while and then drive over to Fisher's. If Levi won't take the money, I'll give it to Miriam or his parents."

"Good idea," said Terri as she looked again at the hex sign, considering the bold, clear pattern. "He does beautiful work. When you see him, ask Levi if he would be interested in doing something appropriate for The Icing on the Cupcake. There's a perfect spot for it on the wall right inside the front door."

"That's going to be a tall order to get home, Terri," said Vin.

Terri gave her husband a kiss on the cheek. "I know you'll find a way, dear," she said.

Piper was used to her mother coming up with ideas and her father's protests as he was expected to implement them. But after his initial complaints, Vin always did as asked. He was proud and supportive of her and of what she had accomplished, with their children, with their home, and with the bakery business. After three decades of marriage and surviving a quarter century with the New York City Police Department and a ringside seat at truly disastrous events, Vin considered himself a very lucky man.

"I wonder if it would fit in the overhead compartment of the plane. No, it's too big for that," said Vin, answering his own question.

As her father speculated about shipping costs, Piper's mind was on Levi and their brief conversation in the parking lot. What had Levi meant when he said the hex sign wasn't just for Kathy and Dan?

Chapter 61

"We'll start with the ankimo and tuna tataki," said Isaac. "Then my friend will have the cod misoyaki and I'll have the shogayaki." He closed the menu and handed it to the waiter.

"I don't know why we even bother to look at the menu," said Elliott. "We come here so often."

"It's my favorite Japanese restaurant in Sarasota. Not that there are many of them," said Isaac. "I wish we could get some more exotic food down here."

"Me, too." Elliott smiled and reached out to hold his partner's hand. Isaac stiffened in his seat and pulled his hand away.

"Come on, El. You know I don't go for PDAs."

"Yeah, but I like to keep believing you'll come around."

"Not going to happen, kiddo. Even if I were straight, I wouldn't make public displays of affection. You can take the boy away from the Amish, but you can't take the Amish out of the boy. Showing emotion is not my thing."

Elliott shrugged and unwrapped his chopsticks as the appetizers were served. They shared the monkfish-liver pâté and the finely chopped tuna and scallions with ginger sauce.

"Remember the time we had puffer fish at that restaurant in New York?" Isaac asked as he tasted the monkfish.

Elliott slowly shook his head as he answered. "How can I forget? I was scared to death. Every time I have liver, no matter where it comes from, the puffer-fish liver crosses my mind. I sat there praying that the chef knew what he was doing when he cut out the poison part."

"You didn't *seem* scared," said Isaac.

"That's because I didn't want you to think I was unadventurous. We had just met then. I was trying to impress you."

"Well, you did," said Isaac. "I'd been in town for only a few months, and I thought you were such a sophisticated New Yorker. I was trying not to seem like a rube."

"You know," said Elliott, "I read that Japanese fish farmers are mass-producing poison-free puffer fish."

Isaac shrugged. "Kinda takes the mystique away, doesn't it? I mean, where's the thrill? Where's the risk? You might as well be eating tuna."

The waiter cleared away their empty plates and brought the entrées. They swapped small portions of the cod and pork dishes so each could try the other.

"It's funny," said Isaac as he picked up a piece of tenderloin with his chopsticks. "On the bay cruise today, they cast out a bucket and pulled in a puffer fish."

"How'd the cruise go anyway?" asked Elliott. "Did everyone have a good time?"

"They seemed to. I have to give it to the bride and groom. They carried on despite all that's been happening around them. I'll be glad when this wedding is over, El. There's bad karma smothering it. And now I'm worried about something else."

"What?"

"The bride's cousin, Piper. I'm almost positive she heard me talking on the phone with you this morning."

Elliott looked puzzled as he tried to recall the conversation. "What's the big deal? I don't think you said anything bad."

"Remember? I was telling you about Shelley and how I was glad she was out of the way?"

"Oh, yeah. All right, you said it. But that's not a crime. It's just how you felt. Lots of people despise their boss."

"You're right, I guess," said Isaac. "But I still don't like that she heard me say so."

As soon as they finished their entrées, Isaac motioned to the waiter for a check.

"No dessert?" asked Elliott with disappointment.

"Sorry, El. But I've got to go back to the inn. I have work to catch up on tonight."

Chapter 62

The Donovans ate a light supper together in the café. Afterward Piper took the car keys from her father.

"We're going to walk down to Nora's and go with her to the condo owners' meeting," said Terri. "Why don't you stop there when you get back? It's at the Robbinses', right next door to hers."

"I'll try," said Piper. "I'll see how my leg feels."

On her way through the lobby, she noticed Walter Engel. He was sitting bent forward in a club chair, studying oversize papers spread out in front of him on a coffee table. Piper walked over.

"Hi," she said. "Working late?"

Walter looked up. "Always," he said, his startled expression changing into an uncomfortable smile.

"I had to get out of my office for a while, though. I keep thinking about Shelley when I'm there. We spent so much time together in that room. She was my right hand."

"I'm so sorry," said Piper. "I really am."

Walter pointed at the papers. "These are the architect's latest renderings of the new building. Shelley had been working so hard to make my dream a reality. Now she'll never see the dream realized. I don't know what I'm going to do without her."

Piper nodded in sympathy. "Can I see them?" she asked, hoping to get Walter's mind on something happier.

He sat back while Piper looked at the drawings. As she adjusted to the scale, she could see how much larger the new Whispering Sands Inn was going to be. The proposed building seemed to spread way down the beach.

"What are these little boxes over here?" she asked, realizing that they were situated where her aunt's condo now stood.

"Those are separate guest cottages," said Walter, his face brightening. "Each one will have two bedrooms, two baths, a living room, and a kitchen, along with its own lanai facing the water. Guests will have the experience of staying in their own private beach house, complete with cable television, Internet access, Jacuzzi, Frette linens, and the world's most beautiful sunsets every evening."

"Sounds pretty out of control to me!" said Piper.

"It will be," said Walter.

"So Aunt Nora and all the others have agreed to sell their condos?" asked Piper.

Walter's expression grew somber. "Not yet. But I hope they will when they realize it's really in their economic best interest. I'm going over there tonight to talk with all of them."

As Piper drove the rental car toward North Bridge, she marveled at the confidence Walter exuded. She supposed that's what somebody *had* to have in order to be successful in business. Piper just hoped that if Aunt Nora decided to sell her place to him, it would be because it really *was* in her best interest.

It crossed Piper's mind that Walter could be wooing her aunt merely in an attempt to get the real estate he wanted. The thought was a deeply troubling one. Aunt Nora clearly cared about Walter, so much so that she was contemplating what it would be like to spend her life with him. After years alone she was finally putting herself out there with Walter. Piper couldn't bear to think that her aunt might be hurt.

―――――――

There were several empty spaces in Fisher's lot. Piper parked the car, took the envelope marked with Levi's name from her purse, and hurried over to the gift shop. The door was already locked. She decided to try the restaurant. When she entered the building, a woman wearing an Amish cap greeted her.

"I'm sorry, but we're closing in a few minutes."

"I know," said Piper, holding up the envelope. "I only wanted to give this to Levi Fisher."

"You just missed him," said the woman. "He left a few minutes ago."

"Oh," said Piper. She thought quickly. Maybe it was for the best. If he had a chance to turn the money down again, Levi would likely do it.

"Can I give it to you to give to him?" she asked the woman.

"Yes. I will see that he gets it when he comes in tomorrow."

When Piper returned to her car, it occurred to her that perhaps she should have gotten the woman's name. But if you couldn't trust an Amish person, who *could* you trust?

Chapter 63

Levi knew the perfect spot. The place where he'd spent so many hours in peace before his life had been turned upside down.

Pinecraft Park was within easy walking distance of the restaurant. Levi couldn't begin to count the times he'd played volleyball and basketball there or the long, peaceful stretches he'd spent on the shore of Phillippi Creek, bird-watching and fishing. The park had been the source of such pleasure all through the years he grew up. Levi was comfortable there.

As he walked to the park, Levi came to the small, squat cinder-block building that served as the world's only Amish-operated post office. He checked out the bulletin board affixed to the outside wall. It acted as a communications hub and was covered with handwritten job postings, announcements of benefit events, and general news to be passed around the community. Levi recognized Miriam's handwriting on one of the index cards, offering to do housecleaning and ironing.

He continued ahead. He could see through the windows of some of the tiny houses where he knew many of the inhabitants. He wondered what they would think tomorrow when the news spread.

Spanish moss dripped from the trees that lined the park. Even in the darkness, Levi could see the shadows of the moss swaying in the gentle breeze. Though the effect was eerie, it was also strangely soothing.

He went by the shuffleboard courts and the picnic area and headed toward the creek. He walked down the concrete boat ramp and traveled a few yards along the water's edge. When he got to the familiar old oak tree, Levi uncoiled the length of thick rope. His hands didn't even shake as he fashioned the noose. He was certain he was doing the right thing.

Chapter 64

When Piper arrived at the Robbinses' town house, the meeting of the condominium association hadn't yet begun. Chatting residents were gathered in the living room, enjoying pie and coffee. Walter Engel stood somewhat apart from the rest of the group. He stared at the floor, seemingly engrossed in thought.

"Oh, Piper," said Umiko when she saw her. "Welcome. How is your leg feeling?"

"Not too bad," said Piper. "I'm sure it'll be fine. Your husband promised me there won't be a scar."

Umiko smiled. "That's wonderful," she said. "Now, come have some pecan pie. I got the recipe when we lived in Georgia. It isn't low-calorie, and it's loaded with carbohydrates, but it is so good that I make it once in a while anyway."

Piper helped herself to a piece, wishing that Umiko's caveat hadn't spoiled the possibility of complete enjoyment. As she turned from the buffet table, Piper spotted her parents and Aunt Nora out on the lanai. She went to join them.

"Did you get the money to Levi?" asked Terri as soon as she saw Piper.

"He wasn't there. I had to leave it with someone at the restaurant to give to him," said Piper, looking for a place to sit. But before she could take a seat, Cryder appeared at the open sliding door.

"We're getting started," he said.

They followed their host inside. Piper saw Walter standing at the top of the steps that led from the dining area to the living room. He began to speak to the assembled audience.

"First I want to thank you all for coming this evening." He turned to the hosts, who were leaning against a wall. "And thank you, Umiko and Cryder, for opening your home to us."

Cryder nodded, and Umiko bent forward slightly as Walter continued.

"You all know that it is my desire to improve and expand Whispering Sands Inn. To do that I need more property. Your property. Property for which I am willing to pay handsomely. Some of you have already seen the opportunity and agreed to sell. Others are hesitant.

"I understand your reticence," Walter continued. "This is a beautiful spot." He gestured toward the Gulf of Mexico beyond the lanai. "I know I wouldn't want to leave it either. But sometimes we get too emotionally tied and can't recognize common sense. The Florida real-estate market continues to be depressed. Who knows when it will recover, if ever? I'm offering you twice what you would get on the open market. With what you'd net from the sale, you could buy another condo on the water, a bigger one than you have now.

"Tonight I'm hoping that you'll share with me why you're resisting. I want to address your concerns and help you see that selling to me really is in your best interest. Who wants to start?" Walter ceased talking and looked around the room.

Cryder held up his hand. "I have to say I don't appreciate your tactics, Walter."

"Me either," said Roberta Golubock. "Your assistant called me in New York and tried to get me to talk my mother into selling. It was outrageous. My mother is totally capable of making her own decisions."

"How *is* your mother?" asked Walter.

Piper watched, fascinated. She wondered if he was really concerned or just asking to ingratiate himself and change the subject. Would Walter really even want Roz to recover? If she didn't, the condo would most likely be sold and he could be right there to scoop it up.

"She's about the same, but she's coming home tomorrow," said Roberta. "Thanks for asking. But getting back to that assistant of yours: Later she called my mother again with some utterly ridiculous and completely false information about me she claimed she'd found on the Internet. She actually threatened my mother that she was going to spread the falsehoods and ruin my career if my mother didn't agree to sell."

"That's outrageous," called out a woman Piper didn't recognize. "Why would any of us ever want to do business with somebody who employs such methods? I for one wouldn't want to sell to somebody I couldn't trust."

The condo owners began to chatter among themselves. Looking ill at ease, Walter held up his hand. "Please, everybody. Shelley might have gone too far. She went off in her own direction on this project. I had no idea she was trying to find ways to force anyone to sell—and I agree, she was wrong to do it. But, tragically, Shelley isn't with us anymore. Going forward, I want all our dealings to be completely aboveboard. I hope everyone can take a deep breath, cool down, and then look at my offer again."

While Walter talked, Piper stole glances at her aunt. Nora's eyes were downcast, and her hands were clasped tightly together in her lap. This had to be so

uncomfortable for her. As if she felt someone looking at her, Nora glanced up. Piper smiled at her
reassuringly.

After she'd listened to the owners vent their views
for a while, Piper felt her attention begin to wander.
She looked around the room and admired the Japanese
woodcut prints precisely arranged over the sofa.
Beautiful silk embroideries were neatly framed and
hung on the wall. On the table next to the sliding
glass door, there was a display cabinet. It was filled
with small carved figurines. Piper realized they were
similar to the ones she'd seen in Cryder's office earlier
that day.

As soon as the meeting was adjourned, Piper sprang
eagerly from her seat and went over to look at the netsuke. Minute scales were precisely carved into a tiny
coiled snake. Every whisker appeared on a sleeping
calico. A writhing dragon licked flames with his jagged
tongue. But the netsuke that fascinated Piper the most
was a monkey perched on a rock as it wrestled and held
down the tentacles of a small octopus. The hairs of the
monkey and the expression on its face were equally
detailed. Even the tiny suction cups on the octopus's
tentacles could be seen.

"That's one of my favorites."

Piper looked up to see Cryder standing there.

"In the Japanese legend," he continued, "the octopus was a physician to the Dragon King of the Sea and prescribed a monkey's liver to heal the king's daughter. But the smart little monkey evaded capture."

Piper listened, amused and amazed by the artistry. "So you identify with the octopus physician?" she asked.

"I guess I should," said Cryder, "but I'd rather be the triumphant monkey!"

Waiting till Cryder walked away to bid farewell to some of the guests, Piper snapped a picture of the netsuke so she could share it with her Facebook friends.

Chapter 65

It was a good night to knock off early. Business had been slow, and customers had been stingy with their tips. Jo-Jo collected the singles from her last table and wiped it down.

"Thanks for covering for me, Lisa. I owe you one," said Jo-Jo as she took off her apron. She glanced at her watch. She had plenty of time to get to Siesta Key. The meeting shouldn't take long. He'd hand over the cash, and she'd hand over the receipt. That's all there was to it.

Afterward she'd be able to go right home. It would be nice to relieve her sister early. Jo-Jo didn't know what she would do without a sibling who was willing to baby-sit for three kids and refused to take any money for it. But after tonight Jo-Jo could do something really special for her sister. Maybe get her a really big gift certificate to Dillard's or Macy's and take her out to dinner with the kids a couple of times.

As she walked out the back door and into the small employee parking lot, Jo-Jo was anxious but also excited. Fifty thousand dollars. What she'd be able to do with that! Buy new sneakers for all three kids, stock the kitchen shelves and the refrigerator, pay off her maxed-out credit cards, visit the used-car lot and look for another car. It wouldn't be new, but it would better than the old clunker she was driving around in now. The beat-up Impala wasn't even worth locking up. Nobody in his right mind would want to steal it.

The car door creaked when she opened it. Jo-Jo got inside and placed her purse on the seat. As she put the key in the ignition, she detected movement from behind. Sensing danger, she felt a rush of adrenaline shoot through her. She started to turn just as the gar-rote was flipped over her head, wrapped around her neck, and pulled tight.

Thursday

Speak of the devil
and you'll hear the flap of his wings.
AMISH PROVERB

Chapter 66

It was after midnight when her cell phone rang. Piper checked the ID and saw that it was Jack. She lowered the volume on the television.

"Hey, you," she answered with pleasure as she pulled the covered elastic from her ponytail and shook out her hair. "I've been thinking about you."

"I've been thinking about you, too, Pipe," said Jack. "I hope I'm not calling too late. I had surveillance tonight."

"Uh-uh. I'm wide awake. I was watching a *Criminal Minds* rerun." She deliberately didn't mention the throbbing gash on her calf or the trip to the doctor's office with Brad O'Hara.

"Nice viewing right before you go to sleep, huh?"

"I've seen this one before," said Piper, stretching out on the bed. "It's my fave, the one where the deranged woman kidnaps the girls and dresses them up as dolls. Fortunately, my man Reid shows up before she really snaps."

"Well, you know those FBI guys," said Jack. "They always get their man. Or woman, as the case may be."

"Not always," Piper teased him.

"Our track record is pretty good," said Jack. "Almost as good as yours."

"You're hilarious," said Piper, "but now that we're on the subject of law enforcement, were you able to find out anything new about what's going on down here?"

"Yeah," said Jack. "As far as the old lady is concerned, some yellow paint was scraped off her convertible, so they're canvassing body shops and gas stations to see if anybody brings in a car with yellow paint and dents. But without a description of the driver, vehicle, or tags, they don't have much to go on at this point. How's she doing, by the way?"

"The same, at least as of a few hours ago," said Piper. "Her amnesia hasn't lifted."

"That's too bad," said Jack. "But the news is better on the murder-case front."

"Really? What?" Piper sat up in excitement.

"The sheriff's department has a kid they think is good for it," said Jack. "And get this, he's Amish."

Chapter 67

Just after daylight broke, Brad trudged through the cool sand to the spot where he'd had his best luck. Tiny fish liked to swim among the rocks that jutted out into the Gulf near the place on the beach where the sea turtles nested. Bigger fish came to eat the smaller fish.

Putting his gear down near the water's edge, Brad glanced over his shoulder. It freaked him out that Shelley's body had been found buried less than a hundred yards away. He was pretty sure the police must be at least looking at him for the murder.

Let them.

Brad rifled through his tackle box until he found his favorite lure. The gold spoon had snagged many a redfish for him. He knew that conservationists encouraged releasing redfish after they were caught. *Screw that.* Any of the suckers he snagged this morning were going to end up on his grill.

He attached the lure to the end of his fishing line and cast it into the surf. As he settled in to wait, Brad scanned the cloudless sky. He caught sight of an osprey hovering, then plunging feetfirst into the water. When the raptor rose again, its talons clutched a decent-size fish. The bird flew straight to the top of a giant Australian pine onshore, where it proceeded to devour its still-wriggling catch.

Brad admired the osprey. It took care of business, quickly and efficiently, without second-guessing. Brad liked to think he had those same qualities.

His brawn and take-no-prisoners attitude had ensured that nobody messed with him while he'd served his time. He had held his own with some pretty mean mothers—hardened criminals who actually scared the crap out of him. But Brad had made it a point never to let on he was intimidated. Those guys could smell fear. And when they perceived weakness, they pounced.

He'd seen one of those guys when he took Piper to the doctor's office yesterday. Both of them knew better than to acknowledge the other. Neither wanted anyone to know of their connection.

Brad felt a tug on the line. He pulled back, giving the fish the opportunity to go deeper into the hook. But it didn't work. The slack told him the fish had gotten free.

As he reeled in the line, Brad stared at the tattoo on his bare forearm. The crying woman, meant to represent Shelley and the tears she would shed for her betrayal of him, could take on another significance now that she was dead.

Piper was very much alive. Brad hoped for her sake that *she* never crossed him.

Chapter 68

Two heavyset women lifted the aluminum folding chairs from the back of their dusty red pickup truck. They carried the chairs, along with their poles, nets, and Styrofoam coolers, down the boat ramp that led to Phillippi Creek. When they reached the creek, the women traveled just a few yards along the water's edge. They positioned their chairs in their usual spot, a place where the creek curved. The location afforded them a good view of any approaching alligators.

"Here we are, Gram," said the younger of the two as she attached an umbrella to one of the folding chairs. "What do you think we're goin' to catch today?"

"Don't know," said the grandmother, "but I sure hope we do better than yesterday. I'm up to here with mullet."

"I hope we get us some bluegill. We can pan-fry them tonight with some cornbread. Mmm-mmm. I can taste it now."

"Well then, girl, put the corn on your hook and get it into that water."

The younger woman did as she was told while the older woman opened one of the coolers. She took out the package of chicken legs she'd gotten from the trash container behind the grocery store. A bit too old for people, but still fine for what she wanted to catch.

"Come on, you little blue devils," she urged as she buried the hook into the chicken leg and cast it out a few feet into the creek. She sat in her chair, leaning forward to peer into the calm, clear water so she could keep the chicken in her sight. Only a few minutes passed before she saw what she wanted to see. A big blue crab was attaching itself to the drumstick.

"Gotcha!" hissed the old lady with satisfaction as she stood up and grabbed one of the handheld nets. Slowly and carefully she pulled in the fishing line. When the crustacean was in reach, she slipped the net beneath it and scooped up her prize.

"That sure is a big one," the younger woman said as she watched the crab struggling in the net. But even as she admired the catch, her eyes caught sight of something moving in the distance behind it. Something swaying gently in the morning breeze. When she realized what she was seeing, she began to scream.

Behind her grandmother, up the creek, a body was hanging from an old oak tree.

Chapter 69

As soon as the breakfast service was over, Isaac escorted Piper and her mother to the inn's kitchen. He gave them a short tour of the appliances and equipment, indicating the counter space that had been cleared for their use.

"Our kitchen is your kitchen," he said. "If there's anything else you need, our chef will help you. And of course you can call me," he said. He wrote his cell number on a piece of paper and left.

Terri used the flat beater attachment of the mixer to blend the room-temperature butter and sugar. While she spent the time necessary to incorporate the air pockets that made the mixture light and creamy, Piper took the various-size baking pans and traced their outlines on parchment paper. After cutting out the circles, Piper coated the entire inner surface of each pan with Baker's Joy and lined the bottoms with the parchment rounds. Then she sprayed the parchment as well.

"Okay. Now what?" asked Piper. "Should I measure out the dry ingredients?"

Terri nodded. "That's a good idea, honey. You know I can't really make out those markings on the sides of the measuring cups anymore. I should have brought the ones I use at our place, the ones that let me *feel* the measurements."

Piper opened the packages of flour and dumped the contents into a large bowl. She took a whisk and stirred to aerate it. Knowing that baking was a precise art, she dipped her cup into the flour, took out a heaping amount, and used the dull edge of a knife to scrape off the excess, leaving the flour level with the rim of the cup. She measured the baking powder and the baking soda with spoons.

Meantime Terri took the key limes and rubbed them up and down on the Microplane. She sprinkled the zest into the creamed butter and sugar, added some vanilla extract, and stirred.

"This already smells like a celebration," said Piper.

Next Terri counted out the eggs, expertly cracking them with one hand and a flick of her wrist. She mixed them into the batter one at a time, so each could be absorbed.

Piper consulted her mother's recipe card for the rest of the ingredients. When she was sure that everything had been accounted for, she divided the dry ingredients into separate bowls and began by adding wet ingredients to the first portion. She stopped at intervals so Terri could mix well before the next batches were added.

"We don't want to overmix or the cake will be tough," said Terri. "The batter should just be smooth."

Wanting the cake layers to be exactly the same height, Piper filled each by eye as evenly as possible. Terri took the padded aluminum strips they had brought with them from New Jersey, soaked them in water, lightly wrung them out, and wrapped them around each pan. The strips would keep the outside edges of the cake from baking too quickly and would allow the layers to rise more uniformly.

Piper felt the pain in her leg as she walked over to the industrial-size oven and slid in the cake pans.

"Good. That part's done," she said, putting the back of her hand against her forehead and sighing. "Tomorrow we'll do the assembly and decorating. Kathy and Dan may have had it rough leading up to their wedding, but their finale is going to be perfect."

Chapter 70

After Isaac left Piper and her mother in the kitchen, he went out to the patio. He was still uncomfortable around Piper, knowing she had overheard his conversation with Elliott. Isaac decided that the best course of action was to ignore it. He would act as though nothing had happened.

Looking up at the clear sky, he noted with satisfaction that the sun was already shining brightly. The weather forecast for the next few days looked promising. The storm earlier in the week had been pushed in by a warm front. Sarasota would be experiencing balmier weather than usual at this time of year.

He was glad for Kathy and Dan. The weather gods were smiling on them. After all the upset about Shelley, they were finally getting a break. Having good weather would also make his own life easier and ensure that the party could be held outside on the patio after all.

Isaac pulled out his cell phone and called the maintenance department.

"Hi, Hector. Will you guys bring over the patio heaters? I don't expect to need them, but we should have them ready to go just in case we need them for the wedding breakfast."

Remembering that some setup had already been done for an indoor reception, Isaac continued with the directions. "And, Hector, at some point you guys are also going to have to bring all the tables and chairs out from inside."

Isaac listened as he was told that the maintenance staff might have to put in overtime to complete the job. He shrugged. "I know there's lots to do just with the routine upkeep of this place. Do whatever's necessary to get the extra stuff done," he said with newfound authority.

Walter had approached him about taking over Shelley's duties as well as continuing with the event-planning responsibilities. It was going to mean a better title and a sizable increase in pay. Best of all, Walter was too busy to nickel-and-dime him. Isaac wasn't going to have to justify every single dollar he spent, as he had with Shelley. Nor was he going to have to worry that Shelley would snitch on him and ruin his life.

Though Isaac hadn't envisioned a promotion as a result of Shelley's death, it was just another benefit.

Chapter 71

As Piper removed the cake pans from the oven, her cousin walked into the kitchen.

"Hey, what are you doing in here, Kath?" asked Piper, smiling brightly. "Isn't it bad luck or something for you to see the wedding cake in advance?"

After placing the final pan on a metal rack, Piper dropped her oven mitts on the counter and went over to give Kathy a hug. Her cousin was stiff and unresponsive.

"What is it, Kathy?" asked Terri, seeing the stricken look on her niece's face. "What's wrong?"

Piper looked into her cousin's eyes. Kathy stared back blankly. "I just can't believe it," Kathy murmured.

"What? What can't you believe?" asked Piper, still holding on to Kathy's arms. "What's happened?"

Kathy walked to a stool and sat down awkwardly. She leaned over and put her head in her hands.

"Is your mother all right?" asked Terri. "Has something happened to Dan?"

The panic in Terri's voice seemed to cut through Kathy's daze. She lifted her head. "No, Aunt Terri. Mom and Dan are fine."

Terri let out the breath she'd been holding. "Then *what*, Kathy? You're scaring me."

"Miriam Fisher called Mom this morning to say she wasn't going to be able to come to work for a while. Her brother, Levi, committed suicide."

Piper recoiled as if she'd been hit. "Levi? The one who delivers the pies?"

Kathy nodded slowly. "He hanged himself from a tree near Phillippi Creek. Some women who were fishing there found him this morning."

Terri looked at Piper with disbelief. "I don't understand. We just saw Levi yesterday afternoon."

"You did?" asked Kathy.

"Yes, he came over here to deliver something to Piper."

Kathy looked expectantly at her cousin. "Deliver what?"

Piper hesitated. Should she tell Kathy about the wedding present she'd commissioned Levi to make? In the grand scheme of things, keeping a surprise didn't seem to matter much right now.

"Oh, Kathy," she said softly. "I wanted it to be a secret. I'd asked Levi to make a hex sign for you and Dan as a wedding gift."

Kathy's eyes filled with tears. "And he brought it to you yesterday afternoon? That must have been just hours before he killed himself. How did he seem?"

Piper thought back. "He was quiet. We were all very enthusiastic about the work he'd done, but he didn't show much emotion when we praised him. And when I went to pay him, he wouldn't let me and hurried off. I went over to Fisher's last night with the cash, but the hostess said I had just missed him. I left the money with her to give to him when she saw him today."

"He's not going to get it now," said Kathy as she broke down and sobbed.

Chapter 72

The garbage collectors tried to get as much as possible of their run done in the morning, before the sun and the heat grew too strong. It was worth clocking in very early in order to be finished in the initial part of the afternoon. The giant truck cruised the city's streets, efficiently picking up the trash of businesses, restaurants, and residents.

Midmorning the crew always stopped for a break, their workday half done. They used the facilities at a convenience store and grabbed coffee, Cokes, and sandwiches. Then they sat in the cab of the truck, listening to the radio and talking while they ate.

"Did you see the Gators last night?" asked Cecil.

"No, my wife made me take the kids out to McDonald's and a movie. She says I don't spend enough time with them. But I think she just wanted the house to herself for a couple hours."

"Man, you missed a great game."

Darrell shook his head and frowned. "I know. Don't rub it in."

"I hope they can keep the winning streak going when they take on Kentucky," said Cecil, crumpling his sandwich's wrapping paper into a ball. He aimed and tossed it through the window at the trash container. "Yes!" he declared as he pumped his fist in the air. "Three points."

Darrell looked at his watch. "Let's get going," he said.

The last streets on the route were on the outskirts of town. The storefronts were adorned with plastic and neon signs. Cinder-block houses sat on small, arid lots.

The Alligator Alley Bar & Grill was a low wooden structure that could have used a coat of paint. Somebody had decorated the front door with a big, colorful alligator, but it had long since chipped and faded. Darkened windows signaled that the bar was deserted at this time of day. The trash collectors drove around to the rear parking lot.

Darrell got out of the truck and opened the door to the pen that enclosed the Dumpster. He stood aside as Cecil expertly guided the truck's two mechanical arms into the slots at the sides of the large iron trash container. Slowly the arms lifted the Dumpster and tilted it backward.

Darrell watched the contents spill into the rear of the garbage truck. Big black garbage sacks tumbled down, along with some loose bottles and cans that hadn't made it to the recycling bins. Darrell's skin crawled as he spotted a mangy rat scrambling to gain traction on the exterior surface of a plastic bag.

"Hey, man!" he shouted. "Hold up!"

Darrell stepped closer to the truck. He barely smelled the sickening odor of the rotting waste. He was used to that. What made him wretch was what he saw.

A woman's motionless body lay amid the garbage.

Chapter 73

"What happens next?" asked Piper. "Do Amish people have wakes and funerals like we do? How do we pay our respects to Levi's family?"

Kathy shook her head in bewilderment. "I have no idea what the Amish customs are. But we can ask Isaac. He was Amish, you know."

"No, I didn't know that," said Piper.

"Yeah, it was a huge thing when he left. I gather that his parents and the rest of family completely disowned him. I think the only one who still spoke to him was Levi. I saw them talking together lots of times when Levi delivered our pies." Kathy looked startled. "I'm not sure that Isaac even knows about Levi's death. I'd better go find him."

"Wait a second, Kathy. Should we still be doing the Jungle Gardens thing this afternoon?" asked Piper.

"It's the last thing I want to do," said Kathy. "I think we should cancel."

"Why?" asked Terri. "It's very sad, but sitting around and feeling awful isn't going to bring Levi back. Your wedding is in two days, Kathy. It's a joyous occasion, and it should be celebrated. Besides, it will probably do us all good to get our minds off things we can't do anything about."

It was comforting to finish up in the kitchen. Piper took a toothpick and poked small holes in the surface of the still-warm layers. Then she mixed key lime juice with some confectioners' sugar and drizzled it over the cake to let it sink in overnight. After unmolding the layers, she wrapped and stowed them in the walk-in refrigerator. All the while, Piper thought about Levi.

On the phone the night before, Jack had said Sarasota law enforcement thought that Levi was responsible for Shelley's death. Did Levi think the police would be coming to arrest him? Was that why he killed himself?

It was hard for Piper to believe that the sweet guy with the gentle smile and real artistic talent was capable of killing anyone. She thought about his demeanor when he'd delivered the hex sign. Levi had been subdued as they praised him and his artwork. He hadn't even wanted to be paid.

But there was something else that bothered Piper. When she followed him out to the parking lot, Levi had refused the money a second time. He'd insisted that the hex sign was not just for Kathy and Dan.

Then who else *was* it for?

Piper took her phone from her pocket. She called Jack, but he didn't pick up, so she left a message.

"Jack, you know that Amish kid you told me the police suspected in Shelley Hart's death because they found his cell phone near where her body was discovered? Well, he committed suicide. I don't even . . . Call me, Jack. I'm flipping out."

Chapter 74

Neighbors had been gathering at her parents' house, ostensibly to offer comfort. But Miriam heard them whispering about "the abominable sin" that Levi had committed. Everyone was standing in judgment of him and "that awful deed."

Let him who is without sin cast the first stone.

Miriam's eyes were red-rimmed, and it was all she could do not to scream. She wanted to run away from all of them and their unwavering verdict on Levi's desperate actions. But Miriam couldn't leave her parents when they needed her most. Her mother was weeping; her father hadn't uttered a word.

She watched as the police arrived and declared they wanted to search Levi's room. As they looked under his simple single bed and rifled through the drawers of the plain pine dresser, Miriam knew what they were hunting for. They wouldn't find it.

Levi's suicide note was already tucked into the pocket of Miriam's apron.

Chapter 75

Piper rode with Kathy to meet the others at Sarasota Jungle Gardens. The original plan had been to spend the afternoon amid the ten acres of verdant tropical vegetation and meandering trails, enjoying bird and reptile shows designed to educate and amaze. Kathy and Dan had thought it would be a fun way to entertain their guests.

"This all seems so silly now," said Kathy as she drove north on the Tamiami Trail.

Piper reached over and touched her cousin's shoulder. "I know it must be so hard for you, Kathy. I'm sorry."

"I've got to get it together and stop weeping and moping around," said Kathy. "I don't want people feeling sorry for me. It's Shelley and Levi and their families we should feel sorry for."

"Does Shelley's family live around here?" asked Piper.

"Her parents are dead, and you know she had a brother who OD'd. She has another brother in the service. He's asked that she be cremated when the body is released. He'll organize some sort of memorial service when he comes home. But Levi's family? That's another story. The whole Amish community considers itself Levi's family."

They traveled on, passing the twenty-five-foot-high statue that stood on the downtown bay front. It depicted the famous kiss in New York's Times Square on V-J Day. An American sailor had taken a young nurse in his arms, swept her backward, and passionately kissed her. The photograph taken at the moment became iconic and served as an inspiration for the giant statue. Now visitors routinely stopped to have their own pictures taken beneath the kissing couple.

"I love that thing," said Piper.

"Me, too," said Kathy as she reached over and turned on the radio. "Were things really simpler then, or did it just seem that way?"

Chapter 76

Cryder took the clipboard from the nurse and quickly signed the release papers. He was running late. Umiko was waiting for him at Jungle Gardens. Not that he had any real desire to go. But she was such a fan of the place. When the invitation had come, Umiko had begged him to take a second afternoon off that week and come with her. This wedding and the run-up to it were taking far too much time.

"All set, Roz," he said as he entered the hospital room across the hallway from the nurses' station. "Roberta can take you home now."

Roz was dressed and sitting in a chair, her hands crossed over each other in her lap. She looked uncertainly from the doctor to the woman she'd been told was her daughter.

"It's all right, Mom," said Roberta. "It's all right if you don't remember everything—if you don't remember me. Everything's going to come back to you. You just have to relax."

Roberta glanced meaningfully at Cryder. "Right, Doctor?"

"Physically you're in very good shape for a woman your age, Roz. That's going to serve you well. Just go home, eat, and sleep and return to your routine. Your procedural memory hasn't been affected, so all the things you automatically knew how to do before, like brushing your teeth or reading the newspaper, you'll still know how to do. I can't predict exactly when your declarative memories, the personal episodes and abstract facts you knew, are going to return, but chances are they will. It just takes time."

Chapter 77

The car eased into the parking space at Jungle Gardens. Kathy reached to turn off the ignition.

"Wait a minute," said Piper as she heard the news announcer's words coming from the radio. "Listen."

"For the second time this week, the body of a dead female has been discovered in Sarasota. This morning sanitation workers found a body as they emptied the trash in the Dumpster behind the Alligator Alley Bar & Grill. The woman has been identified as thirty-four-year-old Jo-Jo Williams. Williams, mother of three, worked as a waitress at the bar. The bar's owner told police that Williams left the establishment at approximately eleven o'clock last night, two hours before her shift usually ended.

"Meanwhile police continue trying to find out what happened to Sarasota resident Shelley Hart, whose body

was found buried on Siesta Beach this past Tuesday. The sheriff's department is asking for help from anyone who may have information about either case.

"In sports, the Florida Gators—"

Piper snapped off the radio and turned to Kathy. "Since I arrived, there have been two murders, a suicide, and an old woman run off the road," she said, incredulous. "When I think of Sarasota, I visualize palm trees and blue-green water, not killers and bodies. What's going on?"

To enter the gardens, visitors had to pass through a low, flat building that served as a gift shop and ticket booth. Kathy and Dan had arranged and paid for admission in advance. Their guests gathered in the reception area, perusing information pamphlets and all the items for sale while they waited for everyone to arrive.

Piper was surprised to see Isaac. He was talking animatedly with Umiko Robbins, gesturing expressively, smiling and giving no sign whatsoever that he'd been informed of his nephew's suicide.

There were quite a few people Piper didn't recognize at all, wedding guests who had arrived from out of town only that morning. Kathy introduced her cousin around.

"Not only is Piper my maid of honor, she and her mom are making the wedding cake," Kathy explained proudly.

Brad came up to the group, wearing an absurd hood decorated to look like the head of a parrot. The bird's beak jutted out of his forehead.

"How do I look?" he asked.

"Ridiculous," said Piper, laughing in spite of herself.

Her cell phone rang just as she noticed Cryder Robbins enter the reception area, his tie askew and his face a bit flushed.

She looked at the number on the phone's display and clicked quickly to answer. "Jack! Can you believe it? Isn't it terrible?"

"About the Amish kid?" asked Jack. "Yeah, it is. But there's something else, Piper."

"What?"

"Another murdered woman," said Jack.

"Wait. The one in the Dumpster at the Alligator Alley bar?" asked Piper. "I just heard about it on the radio."

"Yes. Are they reporting that the cops think it's directly related to Shelley Hart's murder?" asked Jack.

"Uh, no. Why? What did you hear?"

"I called down there to see what I could find out about Levi Fisher and his suicide, if that's what it even was. They didn't find a note. Anyway, my source told me that there was a newspaper article about Shelley's murder tucked into the dead waitress's car visor. It seems she circled the part about Shelley last being seen at the Whispering Sands Inn. She crossed that out and scribbled 'AA B&G' in the margin."

"What?" Piper exclaimed, loud enough to attract the attention of the others in the reception area. Her mind fired rapidly. What if the waitress had seen Shelley at the bar? Could she have served Shelley and perhaps someone she was with? Did Shelley's killer realize that the waitress could identify him? Could that be the reason she was killed and tossed into the garbage container?

Piper took the phone away from her face. All eyes turned toward her as she called out, "Can someone tell me where the Alligator Alley Bar & Grill is?"

Brad stepped forward. "Yeah, it's way out on Bahia Vista, past Pinecraft. It's a dump, lots of lowlifes, but they have great burgers."

Piper spoke into the phone again. "So what do the police know? Does anybody at the bar remember seeing Shelley?"

"Nobody yet," said Jack. "But the place doesn't really get hopping till dark. Tonight somebody might remember something. Meanwhile they're looking through credit-card receipts to see if they can find any-thing that connects to Shelley."

"Jack, apparently Alligator Alley is a dive. I'm not sure the customers are going to be jazzed about coop-erating with the police. Maybe if somebody who isn't a cop went over there and asked around—"

Jack cut her off. "Don't even think about it, Piper," he said adamantly.

"Come on, Jack. It's no big deal," she said. "I have some free time tonight. I could just go get a burger and see what happens."

"I mean it, Piper. Do *not* go there! Understand?"

Chapter 78

*T*he moment Piper called out, asking where the Alligator Alley Bar & Grill was, his antennae registered danger. Slowly, unobtrusively, he moved closer to her and listened.

"Maybe if somebody who isn't a cop went over there and asked around . . ."

What was that nosy bitch thinking?

"I have some free time tonight. I could just go get a burger and see what happens."

Damn her. Piper just might be able to weasel something out of somebody. When he took the credit-card receipt and cell phone from the waitress's purse after he killed her, he thought he had removed anything that could connect him with Shelley. Sure, the credit-card company had the information in their system, but if the police checked, it would show simply that he'd been at the bar. It couldn't prove he'd been with Shelley. Only an eyewitness could make that connection.

But what if somebody else at the bar had noticed him with Shelley that night? Or what if the waitress had told somebody that she was meeting him to extort money in exchange for her silence? If Piper asked around at the bar, she might find out something. In a place like the Alligator Alley Bar & Grill, Piper was more likely to come up with information than the cops were.

As Piper ended the phone call, he stepped away. Pretending to be very interested in the collection of tropical animal toys on sale, he waited as everyone began filing through the admission portal. Glancing around, he made certain that nobody was looking at him. He grabbed a rubber alligator from the display bin, stuffed it into his pocket, and followed the others into the gardens.

Chapter 79

"Who knows the difference between an alligator and a crocodile?"

The spectators who were gathered in the bleachers around the shallow pool glanced at one another to see if anyone could respond to the guide's question. When everyone remained silent, Dan answered.

"First of all, they're from different families of crocodilians. Alligators and caimans are from the Alligatoridae family, while crocodiles are from the Crocodylidae family."

"Hey, Dan!" shouted Brad. "Speak English."

Everyone laughed.

Vin raised his hand. "Alligators have more rounded jaws. Crocodiles have more pointed ones."

"That's right," said the guide. She pointed to the ferocious-looking reptiles in the pool. "See, the long, narrow, V-shaped snout of the crocodile is very different from the alligator's wider, U-shaped one. Because of their jaw shapes, the teeth of an alligator's lower jaw tend to be hidden. On crocodiles they're visible."

Brad called out again. "Either one can do the job. Those babies will rip you to shreds."

After the show the guide invited anybody who wanted to hold one of the baby alligators. "Don't worry," she said. "It's safe—the gator's jaw is taped shut."

As they got up from the bleachers, most of the spectators merely stopped to look at the small alligator. A few reached out and touched it. Piper was the only one who took it in her arms and held it, feeling its snakelike skin and spiky scutes. Vin frowned as he took a picture for her with her cell phone.

"Thanks, Dad," she said. "I'm putting that on Facebook immediately."

"That was brave of you, Piper," said Umiko as the group traveled on to the next exhibit. "I have no desire whatsoever to hold one of those things."

"Not so brave when the snout is taped shut," said Piper, fiddling with her phone as she walked. "It wasn't exactly alligator wrestling. Still, it's a great picture. Look." She held up the phone for Umiko.

"I'm going to put it up now," said Piper as she began pressing buttons on her phone.

"What do you mean, 'put it up'?" asked Umiko.

"On Facebook," said Piper. "I post it on Facebook so all the people I'm friends with can see it. Then they make comments on the picture and we all get into some back-and-forth online."

"You do that?"

"Mm-hmm. One person writes a comment, and then another responds, then another and another. It's fun."

"So you just put up pictures?" asked Umiko.

"Not always," said Piper. "Sometimes I just post something I'm thinking about or something that happened to me. I post a picture when I have one I'm into. Like this picture of me and the alligator. Last night I took a picture of that netsuke at your house and posted it. The one with the monkey and the octopus?"

Umiko's brow furrowed. "Oh, Piper. I wonder if you should have done that. I wouldn't want thieves to come to our house. The netsuke are very valuable, you know."

"Don't worry," said Piper, feeling bad that she had upset Umiko. "Nobody knows where I took the picture. But if it really bothers you, I'll take that picture down."

As they reached the reptile house, Piper hesitated while Umiko entered with her husband.

"I heard that," said Vin, shaking his head. "When are you going to learn, Piper?"

"Learn what?"

"To respect people's privacy."

"Oh, come on, Dad. I *do* respect people's privacy."

"Lovey, I'm just saying you have a very bad habit of sticking your nose where it doesn't belong."

The flamingos were incredible. The flock of bright pink- and coral-colored birds roamed freely on the sweeping green lawn and waded in the large, open lagoon. Piper was mesmerized by their striking feathers, their graceful long necks, and their stiltlike legs.

"How do they do that?" Piper asked of no one in particular. "The way they stand on one leg and tuck the other one beneath their body. I'm telling my yoga instructor that we need to start calling the 'eagle' pose the 'flamingo' instead."

"No one's really sure why they do that," said Dan as he walked up beside her. "Some think flamingos have the ability to make half their bodies go into a state of sleep, and when one side is rested, the flamingo will swap legs and then let the other half sleep."

He reached into his pocket and pulled out some coins. "Want to feed them?"

"Sure," said Piper, watching while Dan inserted the quarters into what reminded her of an old gum-ball machine. Small feed pellets poured out.

"Oh, wow," she said as the flamingos walked right up and nibbled the pellets out of her hand. As she giggled at the feel of their curved beaks, Piper looked up and saw Isaac staring at her. When the pellets were all gone, she went over to him.

"Isaac, I just wanted to say that I'm so sorry about Levi. I didn't know that you and he were related until Kathy told me today."

"Thank you," said Isaac. He shrugged and shook his head. "I guess it hasn't fully hit me yet. Levi was such a sweet kid, but he had a troubled soul. I think that whole *rumspringa* experience became overwhelming. Though he never told me so, I think he probably couldn't face the idea of breaking the news to his family that he didn't want to be Amish. And he didn't want to live a life of shunning. I know too well how gut-wrenching and hopeless those feelings can be."

Piper nodded in sympathy. She was aware that the police had found Levi's cell phone near Shelley Hart's grave, but she wasn't about to bring up the possibility that Levi had killed himself because he was a murder suspect.

Chapter 80

Nora and Walter walked along the winding paths, quietly enjoying the wildly overgrown paradise. Royal palms, banana trees, staghorn ferns, various cacti, strangler figs, bald cypress, and all manner of exotic plants flourished in the botanical garden.

"Will you look at that bulrush?" said Walter, marveling at the tall stalks and the full, feathery heads. "You know, Nora, that fluffy, pollenlike stuff can be crushed and separated from the rest of the plant and used as medicine to stop bleeding."

"Is that so?" asked Nora absentmindedly.

"Yes. You can buy it at Asian markets. The Eastern world is so beyond the West on holistic and herbal healing. I'd rather take something natural than chemical any day, wouldn't you?"

"I suppose so, Walter."

He stared at her. Nora was usually so enthusiastic and eager to talk. All afternoon she'd been taciturn and standoffish. He decided to try another approach.

"I'm hot and thirsty," he said. "Let's go get something."

They walked together to the Flamingo Café.

"What will it be?" asked Walter, looking up at the menu board.

"I'll have ice cream," answered Nora. "Chocolate. I'll wait at that picnic table."

When he brought the refreshments over, Walter blurted out, "Okay, Nora, what's wrong?"

"Nothing."

He sat on the wooden bench. "Please don't say 'Nothing.' You've barely said a word to me all day."

Nora looked directly into his eyes. "All right, if you want to know the truth, I'm very worried, Walter."

"I knew it," he said adamantly. "I knew that something was bothering you. What?"

She spoke softly. "I don't know if I can trust you, Walter. I'm afraid that you aren't the man I thought you were."

He recoiled as if struck. "What do you mean?" he asked in disbelief.

Nora stuck the plastic spoon into her ice cream and pushed the cup away. She crossed her arms and leaned forward. "When I heard at the condo meeting last night that blackmail was being used to get people to sell you their property, I felt sick to my stomach."

"But didn't you also hear me say that I knew nothing about it?" he asked with urgency in his voice. "That was something Shelley cooked up all on her own. I didn't have anything to do with it."

Nora shook her head slowly. "I know you, Walter. You're very savvy. You didn't become so successful by not being aware of what your employees were doing."

"Not this time, Nora. You have to believe me. I didn't know."

Nora narrowed her eyes as she assessed him. "You swear you weren't involved, that you didn't condone it?"

Walter took her hand. "These months with you have been the happiest I can ever remember. You have to know I wouldn't do anything to jeopardize our relationship. You mean too much to me."

Chapter 81

The tropical-bird show starred Frosty, the high-wire-balancing, bicycling septuagenarian cockatoo who in his younger days had been on *The Ed Sullivan Show.* There was an African gray parrot with an ample vocabulary and a very evil laugh. One by one, all kinds of different gorgeous birds were brought out by the trainer, who put them through their paces and explained their habits and habitats. The crowd in the amphitheater oohed, aahed, and applauded with enthusiasm.

"These beautiful and very smart birds have been rescued or donated," explained the trainer as he stood on the stage with a jewel-toned parrot on his arm. "In fact, many of the animals here at Sarasota Jungle Gardens had been abused, injured, or rescued from inhumane conditions before they came to us. Some outgrew or outlived their owners. All of them are checked out by our vets, inoculated, and put on special diets. They will have sanctuary here for the rest of their lives."

At the end of the show, the trainer invited the audience to come to the stage for a closer look at the birds. Piper grabbed her iPhone from her purse and hurried down the steps, joining the others who had gathered around. As she snapped pictures, her attention was focused on the birds. She had no inkling that a man was dropping something into the purse she'd left on the floor beside her seat.

Chapter 82

Isaac drove to his spot in the employee parking area on the southern side of the inn. He saw a young woman in a blue dress and a white bonnet sitting on a trike near the kitchen entrance. He was stunned when he recognized Miriam.

She straightened when she saw Isaac, got off the trike, and ran to her estranged uncle.

"I am so sorry," she whispered as she hugged him.

"Me, too," said Isaac, holding on to her tightly. He was caught off guard by Miriam's sudden affection. "I can't believe Levi's gone."

Miriam pulled away a bit and looked into Isaac's face. "Yes, I am heartbroken about Levi. But it is only now that I understand how horrible it was for you when you left. I am sorry for what *you* have been put through, Uncle Isaac. What I and everyone else did to you. I never fully realized how painful it was to be shunned, to know that everyone was judging you and disapproving of you and ganging up on you. Just like they are doing to Levi now. I cannot stand what they are saying about him in Pinecraft."

Isaac nodded. "I really appreciate that, Miriam. But for me all that is ancient history. I have another life now, and I never miss the Plain ways. I guess you don't fully get over being ostracized, but mostly I just wished the people I cared about could be part of my life. Your brother was the only one who dared."

"I know," said Miriam, sniffling. "Levi was such a good person. I could tell he was struggling with something earlier this week. I just assumed it was *rumspringa* and that he wanted to leave us."

Isaac put his hand up in protest. "Wait, Miriam. I may not be Amish anymore, but I never tried to influence him to leave."

Miriam brushed a tear off her cheek. "I know that now. Levi did not kill himself because he did not want to be Amish. He killed himself because . . ." Miriam began to sob uncontrollably.

"What, Miriam? What is it?" asked Isaac.

After a few minutes, Miriam gained control of herself and reached into her apron pocket. "I want you to hold on to this," she said.

Isaac took a folded paper from her.

"It is Levi's note," she said as he opened it.

The handwriting on the lined paper was clear and meticulous, as if Levi didn't want there to be any possibility of doubt that anything would be misread or misinterpreted. There was no salutation.

I KILLED SHELLEY HART AND I CANNOT LIVE WITH THE GUILT. IT IS BETTER FOR EVERYONE IF I LEAVE THIS WORLD.

Isaac looked up from the page. He said nothing.

"I do not want Levi's memory tarnished or my parents to be mortified any further," said Miriam. "Bad enough their son took his own life, but to find out he was a murderer? How could they survive that? I want you to hold on to it, Uncle Isaac. I want to be able to truthfully say I do not have it."

"Yes, you should be kept out of it, Miriam. Levi would want it that way."

As he folded the note and put it into his pocket, Isaac wasn't sure what he was going to do with it. But for the first time since he'd left the Amish world behind, he started weeping.

Chapter 83

The Gulf of Mexico beckoned invitingly as Piper stood with her parents on the Whispering Sands patio. It had been a long day, what with getting up early to bake the cake, spending the afternoon in the heat at Jungle Gardens, and, most of all, hearing about Levi's suicide and the murder of the waitress who seemed to be somehow tied to Shelley's death.

"Want to go for a little swim with me?" Piper asked her parents.

"I don't think so, sweetheart," said Terri. "I just want to go to our room and relax for a while."

"Me, too," said Vin. "But you really shouldn't go into the water now, Piper. It's feeding time, and you have that cut on your leg. Sharks are attracted to blood."

"Dad. Seriously. Sharks?"

"They're out there, Piper."

"I haven't heard of any shark attacks on Siesta Beach."

"You can't be too careful."

"Really? I didn't know that," Piper quipped. When she saw her father's brow furrow, she softened. "I'll be careful, Dad. I promise."

She walked them to their room and then traveled on to the end of the long hallway. When she got to her door, Piper opened her purse. Reaching in for the room's key card, she felt something cool and slimy. She immediately pulled out her hand.

"What the . . . ?"

Piper yanked the sides of the bag apart and stared in at the contents. Two beady little eyes stared up at her. Instantly she dropped the purse on the floor and retreated several steps. Her heart pounded as she waited to see if whatever was in there came out.

She detected no movement. Piper inched forward and finally got up the courage to reach down and pick up the purse. She held it out from her body as she turned it upside down and emptied its contents on the floor. Her wallet, brush, tissues, lip gloss, and key card came tumbling out. Some dark reptilian creature with a long notched tail plopped down on top of the pile.

"Ugh!" She grimaced, drawing back again. "What *is* that?"

She peered long and hard, eventually realizing that not only was the creature not moving, it was not alive at all. It was a rubber alligator, a toy.

Piper shook her head, wondering who would think that this was funny and trying to figure out when the alligator could have been put in her purse.

Hilarious.

She picked up the toy, marveling at how lifelike it looked. The skin even felt similar to that of the little alligator she'd held at Jungle Gardens that afternoon. But unlike the living reptile, which had had its snout taped shut, the replica's mouth could be opened.

There was something at the back of its throat!

Piper reached in and pulled it out. A piece of paper had been wadded into a little ball and stuffed in the alligator's jaws.

Withdrawing the crumpled ball, Piper flattened out the paper and stared at the word written in jagged, angry-looking script. PIPER.

Chapter 84

The server placed a gin and tonic on the table in front of Kathy and a beer in front of Dan. The couple held hands as they sat in the outdoor seating area at Marina Jack's and gazed at the red-tinged sky.

"It looks like it's going to be a beautiful sunset tonight," said Dan. "And we're supposed to have great days tomorrow and Saturday. Our wedding day is going to be perfect, Kath."

"I'm glad Piper got a ride back to Whispering Sands with her parents," said Kathy. "It gives us a chance to talk."

He looked at her, sensing by her tone that she was about to discuss something serious. Dan took a swallow of beer and waited.

"Dan, do you think we should go ahead with the wedding right now?"

Dan leaned forward, his dark eyes opened wide. "What do you mean? Everything is all set. People have traveled from miles away to get here. We've been planning it for months."

"That was before Shelley." Kathy took a sip of her drink. "And before Levi and Roz."

"Oh, yeah, and let's not forget the waitress at Alligator Alley," Dan said sarcastically. "Hold on a minute, let me call the sheriff and see if there's any new development that could make us cancel the most important day in our lives."

"Don't be angry."

Dan dropped her hand and hit the table with his fist. "Damn it, Kathy. I *am* angry. I'm furious that all this is going on just as our wedding is about to happen. But I was thinking, in spite of it all, that you'd still want to get married."

Kathy flinched. "I do," she said softly. "It's just not the way I wanted it to happen."

"So now what? We call it off because a few things haven't gone our way?"

"A *few* things, Dan?"

Dan took a deep breath and tried to compose himself. "Look, sweetheart," he said, clasping her hand again and looking into her brown eyes. "Sometimes the tragic and unexpected will happen. The most important thing is that we love each other, Kathy. I feel pretty confident that we'll have lots of happiness along the road, but our love can see us through the worst times. I guess this is our first test."

Chapter 85

The air was cooling down, and a gentle breeze was flowing in from the Gulf. Piper spread her towel on the sand and adjusted the top of her bikini. As she stuck her foot in the water, she wondered if she really wanted to take a swim after all.

Then she thought of that Katharine Hepburn bio she'd read. Apparently Hepburn really enjoyed swimming in frigid temperatures almost daily. She also took cold baths at night.

If Kate could take the Long Island Sound in March, I can do the Gulf of Mexico in February, Piper thought.

Bracing herself, she made her way into the surf. She inhaled deeply and dove beneath an incoming wave.

The initial shock was jolting. She winced as the salt water hit the cut on her leg. But as her body quickly adjusted to the water temperature, Piper felt better. An invigorating swim was what she needed to melt away the stress of the day.

She took long strokes, swimming parallel to the beach. When she began to feel uneasy at how far she was from Whispering Sands and the possibility of anyone's seeing her if she got into trouble, she turned around and swam back toward the inn. She kicked harder, knowing that she hadn't exercised all week and had been eating way too much sugar.

Thoughts raced in her mind, one after another.

The Amish pies.

Levi.

Shelley.

The waitress.

Three people dead.

And an elderly woman attacked. Why? Because she knew too much?

Flipping over, Piper floated on her back, staring up at the darkening sky. Who had stuck the alligator into her bag? She tried to remember. The only time she'd been parted from the purse was at the bird show when she went down to take pictures. If the creepy toy had been placed in it then, it meant that someone with them in the park this afternoon had done it. Had someone felt that Piper needed to be scared off? Could that person be Shelley Hart's killer?

If the alligator was supposed to be a warning of some kind, the threat was accomplishing just the opposite of what was intended. Piper got out of the water feeling emboldened and defiant. She was going to go to the Alligator Alley Bar & Grill and see what she could find out.

There was a problem, though. She needed a car but didn't dare tell her parents her destination. They would go out of their minds.

Piper dried off, knowing exactly which person she was going to call. It surprised her.

Chapter 86

"What's the matter?" asked Terri. "Don't you like your shrimp?"

"It's fine," said Piper.

"Then why aren't you eating it?" asked Vin as he reached over to Piper's plate, speared a shrimp with his fork and popped it into his mouth.

"Vin, your cholesterol," Terri warned.

"Yeah, but it's low in fat and a good source of omega-3s." Vin smiled with satisfaction.

Piper couldn't wait for dinner to be over. She appeared to be listening to her parents' chatter about Jungle Gardens, but her mind was elsewhere. There was no way she was going to tell them about the warning she'd found in her purse.

When the conversation turned to the wedding, her father mentioned, once again, how wrong it was that

Kathy and Dan were getting married by a justice of the peace.

Piper finally spoke. "They asked the priest," she said. "But he wouldn't perform the ceremony on the beach."

"So what's more important?" asked Vin. "Getting married on the beach or getting married in God's house by God's minister on earth?"

"I think God will be fine with it either way," said Piper.

"Yeah? Then why is all this crap happening?" asked Vin. "Ever think God is trying to register his disapproval?"

"Um . . . am I on camera?" she asked. "That's completely ridiculous, Dad."

"Is it? I wonder."

"What happened to your 'totally random' theory?" asked Piper. "Just the other night, you were saying that Kathy and Dan's meeting on the turtle-nesting beach was a totally random event. When I said it was fated, you scoffed."

"That was different."

"Why?"

Vin paused and then shrugged as he answered. "Because I said so."

What are we going to do now?" asked Terri as they left the restaurant. "Want to catch a movie?"

"You guys go," said Piper. "I'm really tired. Would you just drop me off at the inn?"

When she returned to her room, she hurriedly changed into jeans and a striped sweater. While she waited for the call signaling that her ride had arrived, she studied the crumpled piece of paper with her name on it. She was speculating on the writer's identity when her cell phone sounded. She rolled up the paper, stuck it back in the alligator's mouth, tossed the toy reptile on the bed, and hurried out the door.

Brad O'Hara's car was the same dark, dirty mess it had been when he drove Piper to the doctor's office the day before. There were fast-food wrappers strewn about. Empty water bottles and used paper coffee cups were scattered on the floor. The windshield was streaked with dirt, save for the crescents cleared by the wipers.

"Sorry," said Brad, as if sensing Piper's reaction when she got in. "I didn't have a chance to get it washed."

"Don't worry about it," said Piper. "You're doing me a favor."

"My pleasure," said Brad. "But to tell you the truth, I was really surprised that you asked me. I haven't exactly been getting the friendliest vibe from you."

"I know. Look: You seemed to be familiar with the Alligator Alley Bar & Grill. And since Kathy and Dan like you, I figured I'd be safe with you. And then you were so considerate when you carried me to the car and took me to the doctor. I thought maybe I should give you another chance."

"You liked being swept off your feet, huh?"

Piper, looking straight ahead, rolled her eyes and wondered if she was making a mistake.

Chapter 87

As they drove home from the Hollywood 20 multiplex, Terri went on about George Clooney.

"He's not just a pretty face. He's a wonderful actor. I was reading about him, and he had lots of lean years before he made it. I hope that same thing happens to Piper."

Vin grunted. "Well, she's had the lean years already, that's for sure. Want to stop at Big Olaf's for ice cream?"

"Not unless you want to," said Terri. "I'd rather go back to the hotel and check on Piper. I didn't think she seemed well at dinner."

"Why don't you just call her?" asked Vin.

"That's a good idea."

But as the phone rang and rang, Piper didn't pick up.

Chapter 88

The bartender put out a fresh bowl of beer nuts. "Another round?" he asked.

Brad looked at Piper. "What do you say?"

"I guess so," Piper shouted to be heard over the din. "I'll have another Ketel and tonic, please."

"Nothing from the well for this one, Tom," said Brad, winking at the bartender. "Another Bud for me."

Piper was disappointed. None of her efforts to talk with bar staff or patrons had led to any helpful information on Shelley Hart or Jo-Jo Williams. Everyone she approached had either been unwilling to talk or claimed they had nothing to share. Piper admitted to herself that she'd been a tad naive and stupidly confident in thinking that she could succeed where professional law enforcement had failed.

Feeling the buzz of alcohol, Piper blurted out her question. "So what's prison like anyway?"

Brad seemed unfazed. "Rough in some ways, surprisingly simple in others. Once you get the lay of the land and understand how the system works, one day just follows another, all kinda blending in. You get into a routine. You don't have to worry about making a living or buying food or paying your bills. In those ways doing time is all right."

"What about the other ways?" asked Piper. "The unpleasant ones."

"You always have to pay attention, and you can never relax."

"Because of the other inmates?"

Brad nodded. "There are some mean bastards in there." He took a swig of beer. "The worst part is, even after you get out, it follows you. It always comes up when you try to get a job. It's hard to rebuild your life, even if you want to go straight."

"Is that why you went into business for yourself?" asked Piper.

"Partially. I'm also better working alone. But the temptations are always there. Just yesterday a guy I knew from inside talked to me about teaming up with him."

"Was it that well-dressed guy in front of the doctor's office?" asked Piper, surprising even herself as she said it.

"How did you know that?" Brad asked, his eyebrows arching. "I didn't even talk to him in front of you. I waited until you went into the treatment room."

"I just had a feeling," said Piper. "I saw you two exchange glances. It felt like you knew each other." She paused before continuing. "What did you tell him?"

"You don't hold back from getting into other people's business, do you?"

"I'm sorry," she said. "It just seems like a natural question."

"Don't worry about it. I've got nothing to hide. I told the guy no, of course." Brad turned away and looked around the bar. "Well, do you have anybody else you want to grill?"

As Piper shook her head, she realized that everything Brad had just said could be a lie.

Chapter 89

Terri kept calling Piper's cell phone but continued to get no answer. When they returned to the inn, she and Vin went directly to Piper's room and knocked, harder and harder, on the door.

"Where could she be?" asked Terri. "She didn't have a car to go out with."

"Don't panic, honey. There's probably a good explanation. Maybe Kathy picked her up and they went somewhere together. Or maybe she's asleep."

"Nobody would sleep through all this banging. Maybe she's sick," Terri said anxiously. "She hardly ate a thing at dinner. Or she could have taken a bath and lost consciousness for some reason and slipped under the water. She could be in there, Vin, unable to get to the door."

"And *I'm* the one who worries too much," muttered Vin, trying to keep calm. Having warned Piper about the sharks before she went for a swim, he'd run the risk of making his daughter a nervous wreck. As much as he wished Piper were more careful, he knew that his protectiveness could be excessive. Though she was a grown woman, she was still his little girl. He'd promised himself he was going to try not to show his worry all the time, but that promise was already hard to keep.

"I'll tell you what," he said. "If it'll make you happy, I'll go to the desk and get a key."

"Good. Hurry."

While she waited, Terri alternately called Piper's phone and knocked on the door. When Vin returned a few minutes later, Walter Engel was with him.

"Oh, thank you, Walter," Terri said breathlessly. "I'm so worried."

"No problem. I'm glad I was still here. I was just about to go home when I saw Vin in the lobby."

Walter slipped the key card into the slot and watched for the green light. He opened the door and held it as Piper's parents hurried past him.

"Piper?" Vin called.

They looked in the bathroom and out on the little private patio.

"She's not here," said Terri. "Where could she be, Vin?"

As they walked back into the bedroom, Terri glanced at the bed and screamed.

Vin followed the direction of her gaze. At first he, too, felt a jolt of fear. But he quickly realized that the alarming gray reptile on the bed was a fake.

"It's only a toy, Terri," he said, picking it up. "See?"

Terri held her hand to her chest and closed her eyes. "Good Lord, that scared me."

"What scared you? What's going on?" Piper was standing with Walter Engel in the doorway.

"Where *were* you, Piper?" asked Terri as she sank with relief onto the edge of the bed. "We were worried sick about you."

"Your mother was worried sick—I wasn't," Vin said with satisfaction.

Piper hated lying to her parents. Now that she'd done what she wanted to and was home safe, she could tell them. As they listened, Piper watched her father pull the paper ball out of the toy alligator's mouth. She decided to tell them about that, too.

Vin studied the jagged script. "*Now* I'm worried," he said.

Friday

Even a saint
is tempted by an open door.
AMISH PROVERB

Chapter 90

FEBRUARY 17 . . .
ONE DAY UNTIL THE WEDDING

As Piper traced the outline of the turtle on Levi's hex sign, she was pleased with the idea that had come to her the minute she'd opened her eyes this morning. She would use the design to make turtle cupcakes and bring them to the rehearsal dinner. They would be a fun way to symbolize how the bride and groom met. Everybody could use a smile right now.

She got to the kitchen before her mother and took the wedding-cake layers out of the refrigerator to bring them to room temperature. Next she asked the cook for cupcake pans and mixed the yellow batter. She knew the recipe by heart. The little cakes were in the oven, already baking, when Terri arrived.

"Hiya, Mom," Piper said energetically. "Ready to do this?"

Terri's facial expression was somber. "Don't 'Hiya, Mom' me, Piper," she said. "I'm still very upset that you went to that bar last night. So is your father."

"That's why I didn't tell you I was going," said Piper. "I knew you wouldn't want me to."

"But you did it anyway?"

"I'm twenty-seven years old, Mom. I don't have to ask permission."

"That's right, you don't. But at twenty-seven, you should have more sense."

Chapter 91

I n his new role as assistant manager, Isaac now had to oversee what went on in the inn's restaurant. He was excited at the prospect of adding more exotic fare to the menu. This morning was the first chance he'd had to talk to the chef about it.

As he pushed open the swinging door to the kitchen, Isaac heard voices. When he spotted Piper Donovan and her mother, he stopped dead in his tracks, unnoticed. They were engrossed in what seemed to be a tense conversation.

He held the door open a crack, straining to hear what they were saying. The mother was disappointed and angry. The daughter was defending herself. He knew that conversations like this were quite common.

But it was the reason for the argument that riveted Isaac's attention. Piper had gone to a bar without letting her parents know where she was. She went to the bar where the murdered waitress had worked, to snoop around.

That was brave of her, thought Isaac. *And foolish.*

Chapter 92

They began their work in silence, but gradually the atmosphere grew less tense as Piper and Terri went through the cake-decorating steps. Despite the use of the aluminum strips around the cake pans, some of the layers had turned out slightly rounded on top. These had to be completely level and all the same height. When stacked, uneven layers could create a sloped cake.

Taking the first layer and putting it on a turntable, Piper picked up a long, thin-bladed slicing knife. She got down to eye level with the cake and held the knife to it as she spun it around. She could see the high spots pretty easily. She cut conservatively, knowing that she could always shave more off later.

After repeating the process on all the layers, Piper measured each one with a ruler to make sure they were all the same height. While she completed the exacting work that required good eyesight, her mother flipped the layers over so each one's bottom became a smooth, flat top.

"I wish I could torte them," said Terri. "But you'll have to do that, too, Piper."

"No problem, Mom. That's what I'm here for."

Piper painstakingly cut the layers in half horizontally, making two equal parts out of each. Eventually the counter was covered with twelve layers on correspondingly sized cardboard rounds.

"Okay," said Terri, holding up a pastry brush. "I'll take care of the moisturizing syrup. At least I can do that."

She dipped the brush in a syrup consisting of sugar, water, and lime juice to add moistness and extra flavor. Instead of brushing it on, Terri dabbed the syrup on the cake, better controlling the amount applied. The cake soaked up the syrup readily.

"So far, so good," said Piper as she took the cupcakes out of the oven. She showed her mother the sketch she had based on Levi's turtle design and explained what she wanted to do for the rehearsal dinner.

"That's sweet," said Terri, "but his death is so awful. Why would a talented young man be so despondent that he'd want to kill himself?"

Piper wasn't at all sure that Levi's death was a result of his anxiety at being a police suspect in Shelley's death. Damning though his cell phone's being found at the beach grave site was, Piper couldn't bring herself to believe that Levi was a murderer. And that he had killed twice? That was even more unbelievable.

Someone else was responsible for the murders and for Roz's crash. Piper suspected that it was the same person who'd left the warning in her purse. Though her trip to the bar last night hadn't provided the answers she was seeking, she was certain the solution was out there . . . somewhere.

She recalled the last time she'd seen Levi in the Whispering Sands' parking lot, when he'd refused to take money for Kathy and Dan's hex sign. "It's not just for them," he'd said.

If the hex sign isn't just for Kathy and Dan, then who's it for?

Chapter 93

Nora poured a second cup of coffee. As she was about to sit at the table and read the newspaper, the doorbell rang. Cryder Robbins was standing out front with a large straw basket in his arms. Red, pink, blue, yellow, purple, and green folded-paper figures poked from the top.

"Umiko made these for Kathy and Dan," he said, holding out the basket to Nora.

She opened up the screen door. "Come in, Cryder. Please, come in." Nora peered into the basket. "Oh, my!" she exclaimed in wonder.

"They're origami cranes," explained Cryder. "The Japanese consider cranes to be mystical and holy figures, living a thousand years. In Japan it's said that folding a thousand cranes makes a person's dreams come true. Umiko's father gave us a thousand cranes for our wedding, which symbolized his wish that we'd have a thousand years of happiness and prosperity."

"What a delightful, beautiful tradition," said Nora as she admired the cranes again. "And Umiko did this for Kathy and Dan? How wonderful of her."

Cryder nodded. "She's been working on them for weeks. She thought maybe you'd like to decorate the wedding cake with them."

Nora hesitated for a moment, knowing that Terri and Piper were decorating the cake that morning. "Let me call over to the inn and talk to my sister-in-law. If we can't use them on the cake, I'm sure we'll do something very special with them," she said. "Sit down, won't you, Cryder?"

"I've really got to get going," he said.

"Please. It'll just take a minute."

He sat down on the couch and waited while Nora made the call. He heard her side of the conversation.

"Hi, Vin. It's Nora. How are you? . . . I'm fine, too, thanks. Can I speak to Terri for a minute? . . . Oh. Okay, then. I think I'll take a ride over to see her. Is everything else all right?"

Nora listened with a deep frown to the answer.

Finally she spoke again. "I can understand why you're upset, Vin. I don't like the idea of Piper at that seedy bar either."

Chapter 94

Piper tossed the spatula into the bowl. "Ugh. I just can't get it exactly right in that spot," she said with frustration.

Terri looked at the tiered cake. "Don't worry if that last bit of frosting isn't smoothed out, Piper. Remember, this is a cake you're making by hand, with love. You've poured a lot of time and effort into it. The cake is your creation, not some perfect machine-made thing."

"*Our* creation," Piper corrected her mother.

"Oh, honey, let's face it," said Terri. "You're the one responsible. Not me. I just gave you moral support."

"Yeah, and taught me pretty much everything I know. So you created this wedding cake, too."

Piper opened the little box she'd brought from New Jersey. "Now for the sand dollars," she said.

Together they artfully placed the sugar dollars all over the sides of each tier. Then, wearing gloves, they gently pressed the sand dollars into the still-soft icing.

"That's absolutely beautiful!"

Piper and Terri turned around. Nora was standing behind them with a basket in her arms.

"I came over to see if you could use these," she said, nodding downward to the origami birds. "But it's obvious that we have to use them somewhere else. That cake is just right the way it is. Kathy and Dan are going to love it."

The wedding cake was in the refrigerator. Her mother and aunt were in the café having some lunch. Piper frosted the rehearsal-dinner cupcakes with chocolate icing and stuck them in the fridge as well.

She mixed up a batch of royal icing and tinted some of it with green gel coloring. Then she spread out parchment paper and piped circles of green. Using a #3 tip, she immediately filled in the centers with brown icing. With a smaller tip, she dotted green spots on the brown, to make the variations in the turtles' shells. She shook the paper on the table gently so that the icing smoothed. Taking up the green icing again, she added the head, legs, and tail to the bodies.

Making a PLEASE DO NOT TOUCH sign, Piper left the turtles to dry on the counter. She would use a black food-color pen to add the eyes before she placed the candy turtles on top of the cupcakes. But that would have to wait until later. She needed to shower, dress, and drive to Tampa to pick Jack up at the airport.

Chapter 95

At lunchtime Isaac drove downtown. He parked his car on Ringling Boulevard near the Sarasota County Sheriff's Office. As he walked toward the building, Isaac forced himself to keep going. He hoped he wasn't making a mistake.

Hearing that Piper Donovan had been nosing around at the Alligator Alley Bar & Grill had helped him make his decision. If a civilian was fascinated by the murders, the police were surely much more intent on finding out who was responsible for the killings. They wouldn't let up until they figured everything out.

He was going to turn in Levi's suicide note.

Isaac wasn't sure that Miriam would approve, but she'd told him to do with it as he thought best. He prayed that she really meant what she'd said and that

310 • MARY JANE CLARK

the action he was about to take didn't turn Miriam against him once again. It had felt so good when she'd hugged him after all the years of shunning.

Part of Isaac wanted to shield his nephew, even in death, from notoriety and scandal. The same went for Miriam. Though Levi's parents and the rest of the family had turned their backs on him, Isaac didn't take satisfaction from the anguish and shame they were going to feel once the suicide note was made public. That was not the reason he was doing this.

Isaac took a deep breath, opened the heavy door, and went inside. If Levi wanted the police to know that he had killed Shelley Hart, then that's the way it was going to be. Now they would have his confession, in black and white.

Chapter 96

It meant driving up Interstate 75 over an hour to Tampa, but Jack had bought his ticket with frequent-flier miles on an airline that didn't fly into Sarasota. A three-car accident stalled traffic for almost forty minutes. Piper gripped the steering wheel of the rental car, willing the vehicles in front of her to move. She wanted to be there waiting as soon as Jack arrived.

When she finally got to the terminal, Jack was already waiting outside the baggage-claim area. Her heart beat faster as she saw him, tall and handsome in khaki slacks, with the blue sweater she'd given him tied over his broad shoulders. Piper pulled the car to the curb, got out, and hurried to him.

"Hey, you. I'm so sorry I'm late," she said, hugging him. "Traffic."

"No problemo," he said. "Just as long as you weren't standing me up."

"Actually, I was thinking about it, but the thought of you all alone at the airport made me misty. I didn't want you to feel that nobody cared."

Jack smiled, fine lines crinkling at the sides of his brown eyes. "That's you, Pipe. All heart."

He hung up his suit bag and threw a small carry-on bag on the backseat.

"I'll drive," he offered.

"Better not," said Piper. "It's a rental with only my father's and my names on it. If we had an accident with you driving, my father would freak."

"Fine," said Jack. "I'm absolutely okay with being chauffeured."

The highway going south was wide open. As they drove along with the windows ajar, Piper filled Jack in on the plans for tonight and tomorrow.

"I'm thinking about giving the hex sign to Kathy and Dan at dinner tonight. I'm supposed to say something to the group anyway, and I thought it might be nice to talk about the symbols on the sign and what they mean."

"Sounds good," said Jack, reaching over and stroking her blond hair.

"You don't think it will be ghoulish or something, since Levi created the sign?" Piper asked.

"Well, it'll be bittersweet—that's for sure. But if you do it right, I think it should be touching. And that's what those toasts are supposed to be. Besides, the kid is dead and everybody knows it. Not acknowledging him or what's happened would seem strange."

Piper took her right hand off the steering wheel and reached up to take hold of Jack's hand. "I wish you'd met him, Jack. I'd have loved to know what you thought of him. He just seemed like the nicest kid. I can't believe he would kill anyone."

"Believe it, baby," said Jack. "While I was waiting for you, I called my contact. Levi's uncle turned in a suicide note today. Levi took full responsibility for Shelley Hart's death."

"No!"

"Yes."

"I'm sorry, but that doesn't make sense, Jack. What reason could he possibly have had to kill Shelley? And what about the waitress who was killed, with the newspaper article about Shelley and the last place she was seen in the car visor?"

"From what I hear, the cops aren't sure about the timing on that murder and Levi's suicide. They appear to have occurred very close to each other. Levi might or might not have killed the waitress and then killed himself."

"Then why didn't he take responsibility in his suicide note for the waitress's murder, too?" asked Piper, her voice rising. "And what about Roz Golubock being run off the road? Levi couldn't have been responsible for that. He didn't even drive."

"I don't know, Piper," said Jack. "But I wish you'd just stay out it. That or go for some formal investigative training at Quantico. Amateurs shouldn't get involved in something like this."

When they arrived at the inn, Piper and Jack walked outside to look at the soft white sand and the Gulf of Mexico. The beach was deserted. The water was calm and seemed to go on forever. The sun was beginning its descent to the horizon.

"What do you think?" asked Piper. "Not bad, huh?"

"Well, it certainly doesn't suck," said Jack. "What an incredible spot!"

"Great place for a wedding, right?"

"Is that a hint?" asked Jack.

Piper blushed. "I meant Kathy and Dan's wedding."

"Uh-huh." Jack grinned. "Of course you did."

They turned to go inside and were surprised to see Walter Engel standing behind them. Piper made the introductions.

"Nice to meet you, Jack," said Walter. "I look forward to spending some time with you tonight."

"Beautiful place you've got here, Walter," remarked Jack as he withdrew from their handshake.

"Thanks," said Walter. "I've got big plans for the place."

Jack glanced back at the beach. "Hard to imagine that it could be any better than it is now," he said. "It's difficult to improve on perfection."

Once they walked away and were out of Walter's earshot, Jack made an observation. "That guy has one limp handshake."

"My father said exactly the same thing," said Piper.

"See? I know your dad and I are going to get along."

Piper smiled, but her gaze indicated that she was distracted.

"What?" asked Jack. "What are you thinking about?"

"I'm hoping Walter is a good guy and not going to hurt my aunt Nora."

While Jack showered and changed in his room, Piper went to hers to make notes on what she wanted to say at the rehearsal dinner. Taking a sheet of Whispering Sands stationery from the drawer, she made rough sketches of all the symbols on the hex sign. Next to each she indicated what the symbol represented. She organized her thoughts and scribbled a few key phrases she wanted to include in her toast.

She took the sleeveless cotton sateen shift from the closet and slipped it over her head. The hand-painted rose print in shades of blue brought out the green in her eyes. The fitted bodice and the contoured skirt fit her perfectly. The hem came right to her knees.

Piper admired herself in the full-length mirror, wishing that the gash on her leg didn't show. But other than that, she was feeling good about her look for the evening. She hoped Jack would, too.

She picked up the sheet of paper with her notes on it, folded it, and put it in the pocket of her dress. Then she went out to meet the others for the beach wedding rehearsal.

Chapter 97

Standing with a towel tied around his waist, Jack sprayed shaving cream in his hand and spread it on his face. He slowly and methodically pulled the razor down his cheeks. Then he patted on a bracing aftershave.

He'd been through rigorous FBI training, had trailed terrorists and brought down criminals. He'd endured scathing cross-examinations by top-rate defense attorneys during trials. He had scores of dangerous assignments and hundreds of hours of undercover surveillance under his belt. None of this had rattled him. So why was he nervous about meeting Piper's parents?

While he dressed, Jack thought about how much he wanted to make a good impression on the people who might become his in-laws. Though he had never broached the subject of marriage with Piper, he was increasingly sure that she was the woman for him.

But he knew that Piper wasn't anywhere near ready. That idiot Gordon had done a number on her when he'd called off their wedding. Jack could strangle the guy for hurting her. Yet Gordon's stupidity had proved to be a gigantic bonus for Jack.

He and Piper had met in a karate class. Eventually they became good friends, going out to dinner and sharing bottles of wine while Piper rambled on about life as an actor and her desire to find a love that would last. Though attracted to her from the very start, Jack hadn't made his move. He was too busy living the life of a young, attractive single man in Manhattan. Then Piper got involved with Gordon, and it was too late.

Now Jack had another chance, and he didn't want to blow it. In the last two months, their friendship had grown beyond the platonic. Still, at times Piper seemed hesitant. Jack supposed that was understandable.

He was treading carefully. If Piper and he were to go the distance, he wanted to have good relations with her parents. More important, he wanted Piper to be able to trust him completely. He wanted to protect her and keep her from hurt in any way he could. Her concerns were his concerns.

He glanced at the clock and realized that the wedding rehearsal would probably be over soon and Piper would be back to get him to go to the dinner. Jack took out his cell phone and called his office in New York.

"Phil? It's Jack. Do me a favor, buddy. It's nothing official, but will you run a check on a guy named Walter Engel?"

Chapter 98

Blazing bamboo torches lit the way to the tiki hut beside Sarasota Bay at Mote Marine Aquarium. The thatch-roofed pavilion sheltered wooden picnic tables wrapped with raffia skirting and crowned with centerpieces of conch shells filled with sprays of orchids. Potted palms and red hibiscuses had been placed around the perimeter of the outdoor room. The atmosphere was redolent with roasting pork and salt air.

"This is ridic!" exclaimed Piper. "We're never leaving."

She scooped a watermelon margarita garnished with a paper umbrella from the tray of a passing server. Jack helped himself to a Captain Morgan on the rocks. "To us," he said, raising his glass.

Trays of skewered beef teriyaki and sweet-and-sour chicken were passed. A disc jockey kept a steady stream of upbeat songs playing. The dancing started immediately.

Piper leaned close to Jack's ear to be heard above the music. "After all that's happened this week, it's almost as if everyone is relieved to finally have something to celebrate."

The music subsided as the bride and groom stood at the front of the room to address the guests.

"Kathy and I want to welcome all of you tonight to celebrate with us," Dan said loudly. "It means a great deal to us to be surrounded by family and dear friends as we are about to make our marriage vows tomorrow morning. To know that so many people are rooting for us and wishing us well is a wonderful gift, and we treasure it. We can feel how much you care about us. Thank you very, very much.

"So everybody eat, drink, dance, and have a good time. Oh, and as a special part of the evening, Mote Marine is keeping the aquarium doors open just for our guests tonight. So feel free to go on in and look around. Enjoy!"

"Everybody, please," called Isaac. "Come see the unveiling of our dinner."

The guests followed him from the tiki hut and out toward the water. They gathered around a wide hole dug in the sand. A delicious smell wafted from it.

Isaac supervised as the pit attendants pulled back plastic sheeting, burlap strips, and banana leaves. The escaping steam cleared to reveal a whole roasted pig.

Everybody clapped while Isaac grinned with satisfaction.

Brad came up to the picnic table where Piper sat with Jack, her parents, her aunt and Walter, and Dr. and Mrs. Robbins.

"Want to dance?" he asked.

Piper turned to Jack. "This is Brad O'Hara," she said. "Dan's best man."

Jack nodded and extended his hand. Piper knew that Jack would be making a preliminary judgment based on the strength of Brad's grip. She doubted he would find it lacking.

"Nice to meet you," Brad mumbled automatically. He looked at Piper. "Well?"

Piper hesitated.

"Go ahead, Pipe. Enjoy yourself," said Jack.

She got up and followed Brad out to the dance floor. Piper wished Brad hadn't chosen a slow song. As he held her close, she could feel Jack's eyes following them.

After dinner Kathy and Dan presented Piper and Brad with their gifts for serving as maid of honor and best man.

"Oh, Kathy, they're gorgeous," said Piper as she held up the dangling earrings. "Are these amethysts?"

"Yes. I had them made just for you." She beamed. "The jeweler helped me with the design."

"I love them. Thank you!" Piper hugged her cousin tightly. "I want you to know how legit honored I feel to be standing up for you tomorrow."

"I couldn't have it any other way," whispered Kathy. "You mean so much to me. Remember when we used to play wedding with our Barbie dolls?"

Piper smiled. "And imagined our future husbands?"

"Yep." Kathy nodded.

"I'm glad the dream is coming true for you, Kath."

"It'll come true for you, too, Piper. You'll see."

Piper glanced over at Jack and felt a surge of affection. "It's got to be right," she said. "But someday I sure hope so."

Spoons clinked against the sides of glasses, signaling it was time for the toasts to begin. Brad stumbled through his, making some questionable jokes that didn't go over too well. Piper wasn't glad about his performance, but it took the pressure off when it came time for her to speak.

"I know that it isn't the usual thing for wedding gifts to be given at the rehearsal dinner," Piper began as she lifted the wrapped hex sign from beneath the table. "But this gift conveys the ideas and hopes that I and everyone else here tonight wish for both of you. So, Kathy and Dan, if you please."

Together the bride and groomed ripped away the paper. As Kathy looked at the hex sign, tears welled in her eyes. Dan held it up for all to see while Piper continued to speak.

"This hex sign was made by artist Levi Fisher. I've been told hex symbols are open to interpretation, but as I see it, the turtle in the middle could only signify the sea-turtle nests that brought you together. Some of the symbols are universal. To the Amish the scallop shell denotes the ocean waves and smooth sailing in life. The heart, of course, embodies love. The tears are the inevitable trials you two will face, but the red-breasted birds remind us that spring and happiness return.

"So, Kathy and Dan, as you are about to take the plunge, please know that we all want the very best for you. A lifetime of happiness."

Glasses were raised in goodwill as Piper realized she hadn't even used her notes.

Chapter 99

*H*e applauded along with everyone else, but his jaw hung open.

The hex sign told the whole story!

Levi might have taken responsibility for Shelley's death with the police and the world. But he'd left another message. Obviously Piper had been studying it, committing the symbols to memory. So far it didn't seem that she'd figured out their true meaning.

Both Piper's snooping at the bar last night and tonight's presence of the FBI boyfriend dismayed him, but the hex sign truly threatened him. Neither Piper nor anyone else could be allowed to decipher it.

Not now. Not ever.

Chapter 100

"Want to take a walk inside and see the aquarium, Jack?" asked Piper.

"Okay. But I'd rather take a walk along the water with you. Alone."

"Let's go."

They left behind the dancers in the tiki hut and strolled hand in hand out to the shoreline. The moonlight glowed on the water, creating a sparkling reflection. The clear night air had grown chilly.

"Cold?" asked Jack.

"A little."

Jack took off his sport jacket and wrapped it around Piper's shoulders. "Have I told you how great you look tonight?"

"Several times, but I can always hear it again."

They walked a little farther, enjoying the view and the privacy.

"Should I be jealous?" he asked.

"Of what?"

"That Brad guy. He was all over you on the dance floor."

"Yeah, I had a feeling that wouldn't thrill you," said Piper. "But don't worry. He's not a threat. In fact, at first I couldn't stand him."

"At first?"

"He comes on strong and kinda scary with that weird tattoo. But—"

Jack interrupted. "What weird tattoo?"

"He's got the face of a crying woman on his arm. And before you say another word, I know it already. Brad is an ex-con."

"Of course. What was he in for?"

"Drugs. But, Jack, seriously, he's not as bad as he looks. He helped me when I cut my leg, and he took me to Alligator Alley last night. He's rough around the edges, but he was sweet as could be."

Jack dropped her hand and spun to face her. "What? Have you lost your mind? You went to that bar where the waitress was killed with that muscle-bound ex-con? Damn it, Piper, what could you possibly have been thinking?"

Chapter 101

The aquarium was almost empty. Very few people were taking advantage of the opportunity for a private viewing. They were having too much fun in the tiki hut.

One man wandered into the building. He smiled at a couple who were on their way out. Then he proceeded onward.

He passed the apple snails and crawfish and stingrays that could actually live in fresh water. He strolled by the horseshoe crabs and the sea stars, the fighting conch and the sea urchins. Cowfish, filefish, striped burrfish, and Florida's premier game fish, the snook.

Then he found it. The plaque next to the tank described the lethal effects of the puffer fish, explaining that those born and raised in captivity were not toxic. The explanation further revealed that the ones in the tank at present had been born in the wild and had continually fed upon prey containing the bacteria they synthesized into their deadly poison.

It took him a while to find the closet where rubber gloves and plastic bags were stored. He returned to the puffer tank, and after one last look around to make sure that no one was watching, he stuck his gloved hand into the water.

Saturday

*Three are too many
to keep a secret.*
AMISH PROVERB

Chapter 102

FEBRUARY 18 . . .
WEDDING DAY

Piper tossed and turned. Finally she gave up and got out of bed. She went to the window, searching the sky for a hint at what the weather was going to be like for Kathy and Dan's wedding day. The sun had started to turn the night into day. There were no clouds looming.

As she stared out at the water, Piper's mind went over the way the night before had ended. After the rehearsal dinner, she and Jack had ridden back to Whispering Sands with her parents. In the car there was only general conversation about the evening. When Jack walked Piper to her room, he gave her a chaste peck on the cheek and left.

This wasn't the way it was supposed to be.

She could understand that Jack worried about her. In fact, she was glad that he cared enough to be concerned. But Piper bristled at the idea of being told what she could and could not do. She could take care of herself. Still, she didn't want it to be awkward between them, especially not today.

She was considering how to make the first move when her phone rang. She pounced on it, hoping Jack was calling to clear the air. But it was Kathy.

"Piper? By any chance did you bring the hex sign home with you?"

"Uh-uh. I didn't see it again after I gave it to you and Dan."

"Oh, no!" wailed Kathy. "You're never going to believe it. I guess those watermelon margaritas took their toll. We must have left the hex sign back at the tiki hut."

"Can Dan call over there and have somebody from the aquarium go take a look for it?" asked Piper.

"It doesn't open till ten o'clock. Nobody will be there yet."

Piper glanced at the digital clock on the bedside table. She didn't want Kathy fretting with three hours until her wedding ceremony.

"I'll go over and find it, Kathy. Don't worry. I'll get Jack to come with me."

The trip to find the hex sign provided the perfect opportunity to smooth things over with Jack. Ten minutes after she called him, he was waiting for her in the lobby.

"I'm sorry about last night," she said. "I'm sorry that I upset you."

"And I'm sorry that I lost my temper," said Jack. "But I wish you—"

Piper put up her hand. "Let's not talk any more about it right now, Jack. All right? There will be lots of time later to discuss it, but let's just enjoy today and have fun."

Jack pulled up the raffia skirt on the last picnic table and looked underneath.

"Nope," he said, standing upright again. "Nothing."

"Do you think someone got confused and dumped it in the trash?" asked Piper.

"Not likely," he said. "It's too big to be inadvertently mistaken for garbage. But I'll go check anyway."

While Jack went off to find the trash receptacles, Piper searched around the pavilion again, hoping they'd missed something. They hadn't.

She walked out of the tiki hut and headed toward the water, wanting to take a minute to get it together.

Tears were stinging her eyes. She hated the idea that her wedding present was lost and that Levi's art was gone. She suspected that it was probably the last piece Levi had made before he killed himself.

As she got to the roasting pit, Piper noticed something that didn't seem right. She stopped immediately when she recognized the big wooden circle lying face-down in the middle of the hole.

"Jack!" she called. "I found it!"

Piper leaned down, reached in, and pulled out the charred hex sign. With great trepidation she turned it over. The front was seared and blackened. The hand-painted symbols were scorched beyond recognition.

"I can't believe this," she said. "Who would think this was trash and throw it away to be burned?"

"No one, Pipe," said Jack as he surveyed the scene. "This was no mistake. This was done deliberately."

Chapter 103

The slice of whole-wheat bread popped up from the toaster. Roberta buttered it lightly and smeared it with marmalade. She put the toast on the tray along with the soft-boiled egg and a pot of tea and carried it upstairs. She knocked on the door to the master bedroom.

"Come in, Roberta."

Roz was sitting up in bed. There was a smile on her face.

"You don't know how happy I am to hear you say that, Mom," said Roberta as she set the bed tray over her mother's lap. "And how relieved."

"There's still so much that hasn't come back to me," said Roz. "But at least the most important thing has."

"The memories are going to return gradually, Mom. Don't worry. You'll get there."

Roberta was encouraged. Maybe it was because Roz was in her usual surroundings again, or maybe it was just that time was healing her, but she'd remembered a few things since she returned home from the hospital. The night before, they had chatted about Roberta's childhood and Roberta's father. Tears had come to Roz's eyes when she spoke of her husband. But Roberta thought even that was a positive sign. Her mother was remembering how much she loved him.

Roz still had no memories of what had happened when she was forced off the road before the car crash. But Roberta suspected that was her mother's mind protecting itself. Maybe the memory would come, maybe it wouldn't. It was fine with Roberta if her mother never had to mentally relive that ordeal.

"Stop babying me, Roberta," Roz commanded as her daughter reached to lift the teapot. "I can do it myself, dear."

Roberta smiled and walked over to the window to look out at the Gulf of Mexico. A big blue heron flew by. Charter boats carrying fishermen were headed out to the deeper water. Large sailboats floated past, their graceful sails fluttering in the breeze.

"What a glorious day for a wedding," remarked Roberta.

"Is today Kathy's wedding?" asked Roz.

Roberta turned around. "You remember that Kathy Leeds is getting married? That's great, Mom!"

Roz ate her egg and nibbled on the toast. As Roberta lifted the tray away, Roz reached out and touched her daughter's arm.

"Do you think it would be all right if I went to the wedding?" she asked. "The invitation is downstairs on the refrigerator. Even if we just go for a little while, I would love to see Kathy as a bride."

Chapter 104

Piper showered and shampooed her hair. As she blew it dry, her somber face looked back at her from the mirror. She was beside herself about the ruined hex sign.

If someone had deliberately destroyed it, as Jack was convinced, why? What message did the hex sign convey?

Going to the closet, she took the notes and sketches from the pocket of the dress she'd worn the night before. Now the paper was all that remained as a testimony to Levi's design. She sat on the edge of the bed and concentrated.

The scallop shell and heart at the top, the teardrops and the birds at the bottom, and the little green turtles in the center of it all.

Levi had said that there were different ways to interpret symbols. What if he'd intended other meanings?

Scallop shell, heart, turtles.

Teardrops, birds.

It was getting late. She left the paper on the bed and got up to put on her makeup. As she stroked mascara onto her lashes, it occurred to her: Could the heart represent Shelley's last name? Was the scallop shell merely a shell?

She said the words over and over. Shell, heart. Shell, heart. Shelley Hart!

Had the hex sign been Levi's salute to the dead woman? Instead of representing the turtle nesting that had brought Kathy and Dan together, did the turtles actually symbolize the place where Shelley was buried? Did the tears represent Levi's sadness and regret about what he'd done?

But what about the birds? What could they mean?

Piper was startled out of her reverie by Kathy's phone call. It was almost time for the wedding.

A bucket of flip-flops stood ready for anyone who desired them. The guests were handed shell leis as they arrived and wore sunglasses as they sat on the white folding chairs that had been set up on the beach. Piper and Brad flanked the bride and groom. Piper wore a short, strapless dahlia-colored silk taffeta dress. The amethyst earrings Kathy had given her dangled from her ears.

With the Gulf of Mexico as a backdrop, Kathy and Dan stood in the middle of a large heart that had been drawn in the sand and lined with seashells. They faced each other and held hands as the justice of the peace officiated.

"If any man can show just cause why they may not lawfully be joined together, let him now speak, or else hereafter forever hold his peace."

Piper held her breath, saying a silent prayer that no one would utter a word. *Please, let this ceremony go off without a hitch. Let this at least go right for them.*

It did.

Chapter 105

When the ceremony concluded, the guests gathered around the bride and groom. There were hugs, laughter, and congratulations. All attention was focused on the newlyweds. It was easy to slip away.

He hurried off the beach and out to the parking lot. Opening the trunk of his car, he took out the plastic Ziploc bag and slipped it into his pocket.

The Whispering Sands' patio had been transformed into a vibrant delight. One thousand colorful origami cranes fluttered in the breeze, hanging from nearly invisible wire that had been strung across the area. Wide-mouthed glass bowls filled with seashells and large pillar candles acted as centerpieces on round tables covered with aqua cloths. Starfish painted with the guests' names served as place cards. The wedding cake festooned with its sugar sand dollars stood on a table of its own, its base decorated with brown sugar to resemble sand.

Servers scurried about attending to last-minute preparations for the guests, who would be arriving very shortly. They paid him little mind as he strolled around the tables, inspecting the place cards, as if he were simply looking for his seat.

The first course, a chunky gazpacho, was already positioned on the tables. He realized with relief that it was perfect for his purposes.

He found Piper's place card and slipped the pieces of carefully prepared puffer fish into her soup.

Chapter 106

Piper was thrilled that there was no head table where she was expected to sit. She was much happier knowing that she could enjoy the reception with Jack. Her parents, Nora and Walter, and the Robbinses were also at the table. At the last minute, two more seats had been added, for Roz and Roberta Golubock.

"I'm so happy that you were able to make it, Mrs. Golubock," said Piper, taking the elderly woman's hand.

Roz looked at her uncertainly. Piper suspected that Roz didn't remember her. And why would she? They had spent only a couple of hours together on what had no doubt been an extremely stressful day for the old lady.

Piper felt her stomach grumble. She hadn't had a chance to eat a thing since the night before. Looking

down at the table, she was tempted by her bowl of gazpacho. Piper glanced around the patio. Several other
people must be feeling the same way. They were already
spooning the cold tomato and chopped vegetable soup
into their mouths.

She took her seat, then unfolded her napkin and held
it under her chin. She didn't want to take the chance of
spilling any on her dress. Leaning over the bowl, she
took several swallows of the spicy soup in quick succes-
sion. She barely stopped to chew the vegetables.

Her spoon was midway to her mouth again when she
saw that Jack was grinning as he watched her.

"Hungry, are we?" he asked.

"Famished. Will you please be a gentleman and start
eating so I don't look like I've just come off a hunger
strike?"

Jack dipped his spoon into his soup. "Mmm. It's
good," he said.

"I didn't know gazpacho had fish in it," remarked
Piper.

"It doesn't."

Piper shrugged and finished the rest of the bowl.

Everyone watched as the bride and groom danced
to the strains of "I Finally Found Someone." Kathy
and Dan looked into each other's eyes as they moved

skillfully with the music. At the end of the song, Dan twirled Kathy around and finished by dipping her backward. The audience clapped and cheered.

Piper snapped a picture of the newlyweds. She was about to post it on Facebook when Jack reached for her hand.

"Come on," he said. "Let's dance."

Three fast songs and a slow one later, Isaac made the announcement that it was time for guests to proceed to the buffet. People queued up immediately.

"Shall we?" asked Jack.

"Let's wait until the line shortens," said Piper. She looked up at the sky where the sun was now almost directly overhead. "In the meantime I want to get my sunglasses. I left them in the room."

"I'll go with you," offered Jack.

"No, stay here and talk to my parents. I can tell they already like you." She leaned in close and whispered, "Don't screw it up. Why not use that fatal charm of yours to cement the deal?"

One of the buffet tables was laden with assorted muffins, scones, bagels, and croissants accompanied by butter, cream cheese, and flavored jams. There was a create-your-own-omelet station and platters of maple sausage, crispy bacon, and hash browns. Quiche lorraine and brioche French toast with mixed berry compote and whipped cream rounded out the breakfast part of the buffet.

For those who preferred something other than morning food, there was a second table featuring mixed green salad with pomegranate vinaigrette, grilled salmon, chicken picante, roasted vegetables, rice pilaf, a carving of roast beef, lobster Newburg, and shrimp scampi. Brad filled his plate, knowing he would be back for more.

As he returned to his seat, Brad noticed Piper walk across the patio. He wished he was sitting at her table. He'd rather keep his eyes on her than on the girls at his. Dan had placed him with some of his friends from Mote. They were okay, but they couldn't stop talking shop.

Brad shoveled food into his mouth as he listened to the discussion about the puffer-fish tank that had been discovered empty this morning.

"I don't understand," said one of the guys. "Who would want to take it?"

"It's crazy," replied another. "But I hope whoever took it read the sign. That fish can kill you, and it's a hard, ugly, terrifying death. Paralysis and respiratory failure with a list of horrible accompanying symptoms thrown in just for fun. Pretty miserable way to go."

As Piper let herself into her room, she felt the start of a headache coming on. She shouldn't have stayed outside for so long without her sunglasses. Wanting to nip it in the bud, she took some of the Tylenol that Brad had gotten for her. As she swallowed the tablets, she realized that her tongue felt weird, as if there were pins and needles in it.

She lay down carefully on the bed, taking pains not to wrinkle her dress. It felt good to get off her feet. *This is all I need. Just a few minutes' rest.*

While she lay there, she took her cell phone from her pocket and posted the picture of Kathy and Dan dancing along with her comment: DREAMS REALLY DO COME TRUE.

It relaxed her to read her Facebook page. She scrolled back to see if anyone had commented on the picture of her with the baby alligator. Forty-seven people had. Some were creeped out by it and said there was no way anybody could get them to pick up something like that. Others were into it.

The picture of the octopus-and-monkey netsuke had brought fewer comments. But one riveted her attention.

I'VE SEEN THAT! AT MY DOCTOR'S OFFICE. AT LEAST HE USED TO BE MY DOCTOR. HE CLOSED HIS PRACTICE.

I HEARD SOME RUMORS LATER ABOUT SOMETHING SHADY WITH PRESCRIPTION DRUGS.

Piper clicked on the woman's picture, and *her* Facebook profile came up. She lived in the Buckhead section of Atlanta.

Where was Piper?

Jack was about to go down to her room to check when Vin asked him a question about what was going on at the FBI these days. He settled in for a leisurely chat.

There was no way he was going to ignore the guy who might someday be his father-in-law.

Atlanta, Georgia.

Hadn't Umiko mentioned that she'd gotten her pie recipe when they lived in Georgia? Could the monkey-and-octopus netsuke possibly be the same one that the Facebook friend had seen in her doctor's office?

Piper's face felt a bit numb, but she paid little attention as she Googled "Cryder Robbins, M.D." on her iPhone. Several hits emerged, among them a story from the *Atlanta Journal-Constitution.* It described a police sting operation designed to catch physicians in the area who were writing multiple oxycodone prescriptions for drug dealers. The drug dealers then turned around and sold the highly addictive narcotics on the street while the doctors were paid huge kickbacks.

Two physicians had been arrested. A third, Cryder Robbins, had been questioned but never actually charged.

Piper's breath caught in her throat. Her notes about the hex symbols were still lying on the bed. She picked them up and looked at them again.

Her heart pounded as it occurred to her. The birds with the red breasts weren't merely birds. They were robins.

And the tears signified what? Weeping, sobbing, crying?

Crying. Cryder.

Cryder Robbins.

Levi had left a record of Shelley Hart's killer.

Vin and Jack's conversation segued from the FBI to Piper. Vin shook his head as he talked about his frustration with his daughter's lack of fear.

"It's like she's just oblivious," he said. "Even though I've tried all these years to prepare her and get it into her head that there is real evil in this world, sometimes she goes full speed ahead without thinking. I'm always worried about her."

"I hear you," said Jack.

As she thought back, it all began to fit. Piper recalled Cryder's dismay at the condo meeting about the tactics that were being used to get owners to sell their places for the Whispering Sands expansion. Roberta Golubock said that Walter's assistant had threatened to besmirch Roberta's reputation with some bogus Internet story if Roz didn't sell.

Had Shelley found out about Cryder's history? Had she discovered the same information on the Internet that Piper had? Had she gone to Cryder with what she suspected and threatened to ruin him if he didn't sell his condo? Had he killed her because of it?

If Cryder was the one who ran Roz off the road, his treachery while treating her was despicable. Roz had seen a man carrying a woman's body into the vegetation near the turtle-nesting area, though she wasn't sure who it had been. But Cryder had to be worried she'd recall something. Roz's loss of memory after the crash had played right into his hands.

Piper knew she should get up and go find Jack. He'd know what to do next. Cryder was out on the patio right now. A killer was sitting at their table!

Her headache throbbed painfully as she rose from the bed. Piper felt very weak, and she realized she was perspiring profusely. The room seemed to spin around her as she crumpled to the floor.

Jack kept waiting for Piper to come back. All through his conversation with her father, Jack kept stealing glances at the door that led from the inn onto the patio.

Where was she anyway? It didn't take this long to get a pair of sunglasses.

"Excuse me, sir." Jack said to Vin. "I'm going to see what your daughter is up to."

Though her brain was firing rapidly, Piper's body was paralyzed, and she was finding it increasingly hard to breathe. What was happening? Was she having a stroke? No. That couldn't be. She was too young for that, wasn't she?

She willed herself to reach for the phone, but she couldn't move. How was she going to get help?

When she heard the knock on the door, Piper was wild with relief.

"Pipe, it's Jack. Open up."

She couldn't answer.

Jack knocked repeatedly.

Where was she?

He pulled out his cell phone and called Piper's number. He listened impatiently as he waited for her to pick up. She didn't.

Just as he was about to disconnect, Jack detected a faint sound coming from the other side of the door. It dawned on him that he was hearing the electronic ring of her cell phone.

Piper listened helplessly as her cell phone rang. Then she heard the sound of Jack's footsteps grow faint as he hurried away.

Oh, my God. What am I going to do?

Her breathing became increasingly labored. As terrifying as it was to be paralyzed, it was even more alarming not being able to catch her breath. She managed only short, shallow gasps, never feeling that oxygen was really getting to her lungs.

This is what suffocation feels like.

Jack rushed up to the reception desk.

"I need a key for Piper Donovan's room," he demanded. "It's an emergency."

"And you are . . . ?" asked the clerk.

"Jack Lombardi." He raised his voice as he pulled out his credentials. "FBI."

The clerk stared at him uncertainly.

"Look, I don't care how you do it. You've just got to let me into that room."

"Just a moment, please, sir."

Jack thought he would go out of his mind as the clerk walked from behind the desk and headed out to the patio.

"Come on, come on!" Jack yelled. "Don't you understand? I said it's an emergency!"

"I'll have to check with the manager, sir."

Jack pushed the clerk aside and ran out onto the patio. He knew exactly where Walter Engel would be.

"I have to get into Piper's room!" he shouted.

Everyone looked up at him with surprise. Vin was immediately on his feet.

"What's wrong?" he asked urgently.

"I'm not sure," said Jack. "But something is."

Piper gasped for air. To make things worse, she was feeling alarmingly nauseous. She knew if she threw up now, she'd be unable to turn her head to expel the contents of her stomach. She would choke to death.

She tried to concentrate, to will herself not to heave. Piper prayed as the vomit rose in her throat.

"Get the master key!" Walter commanded the clerk. "Now!"

"I'll come with you," said Cryder as Walter rose from the table to accompany Jack to Piper's room. The men hurried across the patio, with Vin and Terri following closely behind.

Jack charged in first. Vin and Terri were right behind him.

As the door opened, Piper was sputtering and coughing violently.

"Dear God!" cried Vin when he saw his daughter lying on the floor. He rushed forward and immediately rolled Piper onto her side. He stuck his fingers in her mouth and tried to clear it.

"She's blue," Jack observed as he knelt beside Piper. "She needs oxygen!"

"We have some up front," said Walter as he backed out the door. "I'll go get it and call an ambulance."

Cryder came forward. "Let me examine her," he commanded.

Piper stared back at him with sheer terror in her eyes.

"Piper!" commanded Cryder. "Can you squeeze my hand?"

Her fingers didn't move.

"Is she having a stroke?" Terri asked fearfully.

"I'm not sure. Somebody go to my car and get my bag. It's a dark blue Mercedes, near the front of the lot."

Jack grabbed Cryder's keys and ran.

Roz and Roberta sat at the table with Umiko. All their other table companions were gone.

"I hope everything is all right," Roz said worriedly.

"Don't let yourself get upset, Mother," said Roberta. "It's not good for you right now."

"Cryder is a wonderful doctor," said Umiko. "If it's a medical problem, Piper will be in good hands."

Roberta looked at the distressed expression on her mother's face and made a decision.

"I think we should go now, Mother," she said. "You've been out long enough for today."

Roz didn't protest. She rose from her seat and said good-bye to Umiko. "Would you please call us later and let us know how everything is?" she asked.

"Of course I will," Umiko answered, bowing slightly.

Mother and daughter walked slowly off the patio, through the inn's lobby, and out to the parking lot. The car Roberta had rented while Roz's was being repaired was in a handicapped spot. As they approached, Jack was closing the rear door of the car in the next space.

"Is Piper all right?" asked Roberta.

"No," said Jack as he hurried around to the back of the sedan. "She's not all right. I'm trying to find the doctor's bag now."

While they watched, he popped open the trunk and looked inside. "There it is," he said with satisfaction. Jack grabbed the satchel, slammed down the lid, and ran. He completely missed the startled look of recognition on the old woman's face.

When Jack got back to the room, the doctor had the heel of his hand in the middle of Piper's chest. His other hand was on top, interlaced with the first. Cryder pushed her chest down and then let it rise before compressing it again. He repeated the process over and over. Jack winced as he heard a popping sound come from Piper's chest.

"Stop!" cried Terri. "You're hurting her!"

Vin put his arm around his wife and pulled her close. "He can't stop, sweetheart."

"Shouldn't you breathe into her mouth?" Jack asked desperately.

Cryder shot him a look. Jack couldn't read it. Was it fear? Anger? Distaste? Was it possible that the doctor didn't want to put his mouth on Piper's?

"Let me take over," said Jack. He set the medical bag down next to Dr. Robbins. "I've taken the training. You do something else to help her."

Jack took the oxygen mask off Piper and checked to make sure there was nothing in her mouth. Then he tilted her head back and pinched her nose. Forming a seal over her mouth with his, Jack breathed in enough air to make her chest rise. At the same time, Cryder wrapped a blood-pressure cuff around Piper's arm.

"How is it?" asked Terri.

Cryder studied the gauge. "Low," he answered. "Very low."

"She's breathing!"

Jack leaned back on his heels. Piper was inhaling and exhaling with short, quick gulps. But at least she was breathing.

The ambulance team arrived and took her vital signs. After putting the oxygen mask on Piper's face, they lifted her onto the gurney and started to roll her away.

"I'll take my car and meet you at the emergency room," said Cryder.

"What are you doing?" asked Terri as she watched her husband enter the bathroom. "We have to go with Piper."

Cryder and Jack looked on as Vin came out holding a paper-wrapped drinking glass. Vin carefully removed the covering and tossed it, then knelt down next to the spot where his daughter had lain. Taking a credit card from his wallet, he scraped up the vomit and deposited it in the glass.

"I want to bring this with us, just in case they need to test it," Vin said glumly.

———

A crowd of wedding guests had gathered around the ambulance. They watched silently as the attendants slid the gurney inside. Kathy stood in her wedding dress, sobbing. Dan's tanned face was ashen.

Brad pulled at Jack's sleeve. "What can I do to help?" he asked.

"Pray," said Jack.

"What's wrong with her?"

"They don't know yet," said Jack, watching the ambulance doors close. "She can't move. She can hardly breathe, and she puked her guts up all over the floor."

It was only after the ambulance and the other cars pulled away that Brad thought of the missing puffer fish.

En route to the hospital, Piper stopped breathing again. Her mother squeezed herself against the wall of the ambulance while the EMTs continued with chest compressions.

"Hail Mary, full of grace," Terri whispered. "Please, let my little girl live."

The ambulance pulled into the emergency-room bay. Vin and Jack pulled up immediately behind.

Two doctors and three nurses were waiting. They flanked the gurney and rolled it inside, listening while the EMT recited the symptoms. The doctors looked at each other and nodded.

"Let's empty her stomach and pump in activated charcoal to bind any toxins," one commanded.

"Toxins?" asked Vin.

"Did your daughter eat any seafood?"

"I'm not sure," said Vin. "Did she, Terri?"

Jack interrupted before Piper's mother could answer. "She never got to the buffet. But she remarked how fishy the gazpacho tasted."

"Well, we got a phone call just before you arrived," said the doctor. "Someone thinks she could have ingested tetrodotoxin. Her symptoms are textbook."

"Tetro what?" asked Vin.

"Tetrodotoxin. The toxin found in puffer fish."

Vin stopped, the memory of the dangerous-fish lecture at Mote exploding in his mind. His baby was going to die.

"What's the prognosis?" Jack called as the gurney was pushed into the treatment room.

"The next twenty-four hours are critical. We'll put her on standard life-support measures to keep her alive and hope that the effects of the poison wear off."

Jack went with Piper's parents to the waiting room, and all three silently sank into chairs. They sat staring vacantly as they contemplated what had happened and feared what might be coming. Several minutes went by until Jack raised his head and looked around.

"Hey, where's Dr. Robbins? Didn't he follow us?"

Chapter 107

Tears streamed down Umiko's cheeks. "I don't want to leave this place, Cryder."

"I know," Cryder said as he gathered the netsuke from the cabinet in their living room. "But we have no choice. It's too dangerous to stay."

While he'd attended Piper, he had prayed she would die quickly. He'd gone through the expected medical motions to cover himself, all the while hoping that it was just a matter of time before she died. But Walter Engel's getting the oxygen and calling the ambulance as quickly as he had and Piper's boyfriend rushing in like a hero to give her mouth-to-mouth resuscitation had staved off her quick demise. When Vin Donovan took the sample of Piper's expelled stomach contents, Cryder knew that tests would show the presence of tetrodotoxin.

They would realize that Piper had eaten puffer fish, and the people at Mote would know that a puffer fish was gone from their tank. The police would investigate, focusing on the guests at the rehearsal dinner as suspects in the theft.

Admittedly, he wasn't the only one there. But investigators would soon learn that the hex sign had also been destroyed that night. If she survived, the police would be sure to question Piper about her memory of the symbols. It wouldn't take long before someone figured out that the hex sign pointed to him as Shelley Hart's killer. Eventually they would make the connection to Roz's car crash and to the dead waitress.

"But I don't understand," said Umiko. "Why do we have to go now?"

He walked over to his wife and took her by the shoulders. "This time I've done things much worse than writing prescriptions. Things that could cost me my life."

Umiko stared into her husband's eyes as she tried to figure out what he was saying. "Does this have something to do with Piper and what just happened at the wedding?" she asked.

He nodded. "And Shelley Hart and Roz Golubock and a greedy waitress who knew too much."

Umiko recoiled as the enormity of what he was saying sank in. She collapsed on the sofa.

"Come on, Umiko," Cryder urged. "Get up. We have to grab what we can and leave."

She stayed exactly where she was. "I'm not going," she whispered.

"Meaning what?"

"Dealing with drug people was horrible enough, but you were my husband and I felt it was my duty to stand by you. But murder is much different. I can't live with the dishonor of being married to a killer."

Sunday

There are lots of ways
to cut a cake.
AMISH PROVERB

Epilogue

Piper's head rested against the pillow. She was pale and weak, but she was breathing on her own. Her heart rate had almost returned to normal, and she could move her arms and legs again. Her parents stood with Kathy, Dan, Aunt Nora, and Walter around the hospital bed while Jack described what had happened as Piper was fighting for her life.

"When Cryder didn't follow us to the hospital, we got suspicious. I went back to your room and noticed your iPhone on the bed. It was still open to the last Internet search you did."

Piper tried to think. "The article about the drug prescriptions in Atlanta, right?"

"Exactly," said Jack. "When I saw Cryder Robbins named, things started to come together."

"And then Roz Golubock's daughter called to see how you were, Piper," said Nora. "She said her mother's memory was jogged when she saw Cryder's open trunk yesterday. There was a shovel in there with a red-and-yellow shaft. Very distinctive. Roz suddenly recalled seeing it on the night the man had carried the woman's body into the vegetation next to her condo."

"The sheriff's department managed to pull Robbins over as he was driving out of the city," said Vin as he held tight to his daughter's hand.

"But do we know exactly why Cryder would want to kill Shelley?" asked Piper.

Walter shrugged remorsefully. "I think Shelley might have come across the information about Cryder on the Web and tried to blackmail him with it, forcing him to sell his condo."

Kathy looked skeptical. "I still don't think Shelley would have done that," she said. "It wasn't about money for her. After her brother OD'd, she became obsessed about drugs. Her testimony put Brad in jail for dealing. I'll bet she went to Cryder, told him what she knew and told him to stop."

"Either way she was a very naive or stupid young woman," said Vin. "She should have gone straight to the police."

Walter put his arm around Nora. "Whatever happened, this is making me reconsider a lot of things. I'm going to cancel the Whispering Sands expansion and just appreciate the place the way it is. I want to concentrate on enjoying life, not business."

Isaac arrived just as Piper's parents and Nora and Walter were leaving. He carried a gigantic arrangement of flowers. Seeing Isaac made Piper think of his nephew, the young Amish man who had taken his own life.

"I don't understand," she said softly. "If Cryder killed Shelley, why did Levi take responsibility?

"Good question," said Jack. "The police now think Levi may have written the note for other reasons. They're trying to figure that part out."

There was something else, but Piper couldn't think of it yet. What was it? She lay there quietly, and slowly the hex sign emerged in her mind.

"Levi left a message about Cryder in the hex sign he painted." Piper recounted what she had discerned from the symbols. "Poor Levi had confessed to killing Shelley in his suicide note, but he left clues pointing to the real murderer in his art."

Jack reached over and stroked Piper's blond hair. "That's another nail in the good doctor's coffin," he said.

Kathy shook her head in disbelief. "It's amazing that we can thank Brad O'Hara, of all people, that you're alive, Piper," she said. "He's the one who called the ER and told them you might have eaten puffer fish. We're so grateful to that big lug."

"Very," said Dan, letting out a deep sigh. "And I think *Brad's* grateful that he had the chance to *save* a life this time instead of contribute to somebody's *losing* one."

As they prepared to leave, Kathy and Dan kissed Piper on the cheek. "Now that we know you're okay, we're going ahead with our honeymoon," said Kathy. "Our new flight takes off early in the morning."

"I hate that you had to reschedule because of me," said Piper.

"Are you kidding?" asked Dan. "Now we can go and really enjoy ourselves. You're all right, and Cryder Robbins is going to get what he deserves. This has been a nightmare, but it's over now."

Isaac had remained silent through the whole conversation. " 'We value the light more fully after we come out of the darkness,' " he whispered.

Everyone looked at him. "It's an Amish proverb," he explained, knowing that at the first possible opportunity he was going to return the sea turtle mosaic to its rightful place at Whispering Sands Inn. Levi would want it that way.

Aunt Nora's Easy but Sinfully Delicious Siesta Key Lime Pie

One 8-ounce package cream cheese (softened)
One 14-ounce can sweetened condensed milk
2 teaspoons vanilla extract
½ cup key lime juice (not regular lime juice, *KEY* lime juice)
Graham cracker crust pie shell (store-bought is fine)

With an electric mixer in a medium bowl, beat cheese until creamy. Gradually beat in condensed milk and continue beating until smooth. Mix in vanilla extract. Add key lime juice and blend thoroughly. Pour mixture into the pie shell, cover, and refrigerate at least six hours.

Note: As you can see, this is not a complicated, gourmet-style recipe, but it seems that everyone who takes a bite of this pie raves, smiles, and asks for more.

Acknowledgments

I stand in awe of sea turtles.

The odds are certainly against them. The mama turtle has to drag herself up on the beach in the middle of the night and dig a deep nest in the sand with her rear flippers, hopefully picking a spot that won't get washed out by a storm or plundered by animal and human invaders. About two months later, also in the dark, the hatchlings have to claw their own way up through the sand and out of the nest, trying to evade the night herons, raccoons, and other predators that eagerly await them as they scurry to the water. Once there, the tiny turtles face the threat of being eaten by larger marine life. It seems a miracle that any make it to adulthood. Few actually do. But after traveling hundreds of miles through the world's oceans, the mature female finds her way back to the same beach where she was born three decades earlier to lay her own eggs.

Books, in a way, are like sea turtles. So many elements have to fall into place as the book is conceived, researched, written, and published. There are so many opportunities for things to go awry. The forces of the universe, mostly in human form, have to be aligned with the author, contributing to the development and survival of the book.

From the very start, until the very last page, Father Paul Holmes offered his encouragement and imagination. Paul was quick to point out if I had my head in the sand regarding characters and motives. His repeated calls for "action" reminded me to keep things moving. His support was crucial and so appreciated.

Elizabeth Higgins Clark, my actress daughter, is the inspiration for Piper Donovan. Elizabeth read the pages for me and pointed out all the instances this middle-aged writer messed up on the voice of a twenty-seven-year-old. Elizabeth made sure that Piper's words rang true. You're a good girl, Monkey.

Many thanks to Kathy Leeds, the former executive director of Connecticut's Wilton Public Library, and Roz and Roberta Golubock, who supported the Atlanta-Fulton Public Library System, lending their names for characters.

Jennifer Rudolph Walsh is a force of nature, and I know how fortunate I am to have her as my agent. Joni Evans, busy as she is, found the time to provide suggestions. My gratitude to both of you.

The professional and supportive team at William Morrow/HarperCollins are a dedicated and impressive bunch. Carrie Feron, my insightful and creative editor, and Tessa Woodward, who faithfully juggles so many, many things, are my dependable touchstones. Seale Ballenger, Kimberly Chocolaad, Lynn Grady, Stephanie Kim, Tavia Kowalchuk, Michael Morrison, Shawn Nicholls, Sharyn Rosenblum, Virginia Stanley, and Liate Stehlik play at the top of their games. I've grown to happily anticipate Maureen Sugden's masterful copyediting. Many, many thanks to all of you and to the others, unnamed here, who contributed their publishing expertise.

For the last several years, Peggy Gould has given me reassurance and peace of mind. I am utterly and eternally grateful. Without her, I don't think I'd have been able to concentrate enough to write this book.

And finally, much appreciation to my beloved Sarasota and Siesta Key, which provide the lush, magical atmosphere perfect for a dream wedding or a twisted mystery. No wonder those sea turtles keep coming back. They know a good thing.

HARPER LUXE

THE NEW LUXURY IN READING

We hope you enjoyed reading
our new, comfortable print size and found it
an experience you would like to repeat.

Well – you're in luck!

HarperLuxe offers the finest in fiction and
nonfiction books in this same larger print size and
paperback format. Light and easy to read, HarperLuxe
paperbacks are for book lovers who want to see
what they are reading without the strain.

For a full listing of titles and
new releases to come, please visit our website:

www.HarperLuxe.com